Praise for *Nebraska*

"*Nebraska* captures a rowdy, changing America. Written with wit and brawny lyricism, in voices ranging from hip to tender, the stories gathered here are as diverse and expansive as the country they celebrate....References to America's heartland abound throughout the book and serve as a central metaphor for what's close to American hearts, what connects us: dreams, myths and possibilities as vast as the Great Plains. Wise and smart-alecky, creaking with legend and crackling with modernisms, these 10 tales are about American obsessions past and present." —*The Washington Post Book World*

"Just as Raymond Carver came to be identified with a Pacific Northwest populated by blue-collar workers, and just as Richard Ford has crafted a Montana full of drifters, so Ron Hansen has carved out his own geographical niche. His *Nebraska* is a distinctive mix of 19th century settlers and 1980's breadwinners, of sudden storms and life-long yearnings, of lost souls stranded in the middle of nowhere. It should put him on the short-story map."

—*USA Today*

"Hansen at his best enables us to believe that beyond the quiet beauty of the commonplace are worlds of infinite variation, more mysterious and sometimes more threatening than our daily routines permit us to sense."

—*Los Angeles Times Book Review*

"Part Hemingway and part García Márquez—Hansen's something of an all-American magic realist, in other words, a fabulist in the native grain."

—*Kirkus Reviews*

"Mr. Hansen's talent for sensuous detail travels very well—to the late 1800's, to the 1940's, to the present day....His language operates elegantly....Deeply gratifying." —*The New York Times Book Review*

Nebraska

Also by Ron Hansen

Desperadoes

The Assassination of Jesse James by the Coward Robert Ford

For children

The Shadowmaker

Nebraska

Stories

Ron Hansen

THE ATLANTIC MONTHLY PRESS
NEW YORK

Acknowledgments

Early versions of these stories originally appeared in the following periodicals and anthologies: "Wickedness" in *The Sonora Review*; "Playland" in MSS; "The Killers" in *The Iowa Review*; "His Dog" in *The Ark River Review*; "The Sun So Hot I Froze to Death" in *The Stanford Alumni Magazine* and *Mirror and Mirage*; "Can I Just Sit Here for a While?" in *The Atlantic* and *Matters of Life and Death*; "The Boogeyman" in *The Iowa Review* and, revised, in *Hayden's Ferry Review*; "True Romance" in *Esquire* and *The Esquire Fiction Reader*; "Sleepless" in *The Paris Review*; "Red-Letter Days" in *The Michigan Quarterly Review*; and "Nebraska" in *Prairie Schooner* and *Harper's*.

I wish to express my appreciation to the National Endowment for the Arts for its generous support.

Published simultaneously in Canada
Printed in the United States of America

Library of Congress Cataloging-in-Publication Data

Hansen, Ron, 1947–
Nebraska: stories.

1. Nebraska—Fiction. I. Title.
PS3558.A5133N44 1989 813'.54 88-24189
ISBN 0-87113-252-4 (HC)
ISBN 0-87113-349-0 (PB)

The Atlantic Monthly Press
841 Broadway
New York, NY 10003

for Julie

Contents

Wickedness

At the end of the nineteenth century a girl from Delaware got on a milk train in Omaha and took a green wool seat in the second-class car. August was outside the window, and sunlight was a yellow glare on the trees. Up front, a railway conductor in a navy-blue uniform was gingerly backing down the aisle with a heavy package in a gunnysack that a boy was helping him with. They were talking about an agreeable seat away from the hot Nebraska day that was persistent outside, and then they were setting their cargo across the runnered aisle from the girl and tilting it against the shellacked wooden wall of the railway car before walking back up the aisle and elsewhere into August.

She was sixteen years old and an Easterner just recently hired as a county schoolteacher, but she knew enough about prairie farming to think the heavy package was a crank-and-piston washing machine or a boxed plowshare and coulter, something no higher than the bloody stump where the poultry were chopped with a hatchet and then wildly high-stepped around the yard. Soon, however, there was a juggling movement and the gunnysack slipped aside, and she saw an old man sitting there, his limbs hacked away, and dark holes where his ears ought to have been, the skin pursed at his jaw hinge like pink lips in a kiss. The milk train jerked into a roll through the railway yard, and the old man was jounced so that his gray cheek pressed against the hot window glass. Although he didn't complain, it seemed an uneasy position, and the girl wished she had the courage to get up from her seat and tug the jolting body upright. She instead got to her page in *Quo Vadis* and pretended to be so rapt by the book that she didn't look up again until Columbus, where a doctor with liquorice on his breath sat heavily beside her and openly stared over his newspaper before whispering that the poor man was a carpenter in Genoa who'd been caught out in the great blizzard of 1888. Had she heard of that one?

The girl shook her head.

She ought to look out for their winters, the doctor said. Weather in Nebraska could be the wickedest thing she ever saw.

She didn't know what to say, so she said nothing. And at Genoa a young teamster got on in order to carry out the old man, whose half body was heavy enough that the boy had to yank the gunnysack up the aisle like sixty pounds of mail.

In the year 1888, on the twelfth day of January, a pink sun was up just after seven and southeastern zephyrs of such soft temperature were sailing over the Great Plains that squatters walked their properties in high rubber boots and April jackets and some farmhands took off their Civil War greatcoats to rake silage into the cattle troughs. However, sheep that ate whatever they could the night before raised their heads away from food and sniffed the salt tang in the air. And all that morning streetcar mules were reported to be acting up, nipping each other, jingling the hitch rings, foolishly waggling their dark manes and necks as though beset by gnats and horseflies.

A Danish cattleman named Axel Hansen later said he was near the Snake River and tipping a teaspoon of saleratus into a yearling's mouth when he heard a faint groaning in the north that was like the noise of a high waterfall at a fair distance. Axel looked toward Dakota, and there half the sky was suddenly gray and black and indigo blue with great storm clouds that were seething up as high as the sun and wrangling toward him at horse speed. Weeds were being uprooted, sapling trees were bullwhipping, and the top inches of snow and prairie soil were being sucked up and stirred like the dirty flour that was called red dog. And then the onslaught hit him hard as furniture, flying him onto his back so that when Axel looked up, he seemed to be deep undersea and in icehouse cold. Eddying snow made it hard to breathe any way but sideways, and getting up to just his knees and hands seemed a great attainment. Although his sod house was but a quarter-mile away, it took Axel four hours to get there. Half his face was frozen gray and hard as weatherboarding so the cattleman was speechless until nightfall, and then Axel Hansen simply told his wife, That was not pleasant.

Cow tails stuck out sideways when the wind caught them. Sparrows and crows whumped hard against the windowpanes, their jerking eyes seeking out an escape, their wings fanned out and flattened as though pinned up in an ornithologist's display. Cats died, dogs died, pigeons died. Entire farms of cattle and pigs and geese and chickens were wiped out in a single night. Horizontal snow that was hard and dry as salt dashed and seethed over everything, sloped up like rooftops, tricked its way across creek beds and ditches, milkily purled down city streets, stole shanties and coops and pens from a bleak landscape that was even then called the Great American Desert. Everything about the blizzard seemed to have personality and hateful intention. Especially the cold. At six a.m., the temperature at Valentine, Nebraska, was thirty degrees above zero. Half a day later the temperature was fourteen below, a drop of forty-four degrees and the difference between having toes and not, between staying alive overnight and not, between ordinary concerns and one overriding idea.

Ainslie Classen was hopelessly lost in the whiteness and tilting low under the jamming gale when his right elbow jarred against a joist of his pigsty. He walked around the sty by skating his sore red hands along the upright shiplap and then squeezed inside through the slops trough. The pigs scampered over to him, seeking his protection, and Ainslie put himself among them, getting down in their stink and their body heat, socking them away only when they ganged up or when two or three presumed he was food. Hurt was nailing into his finger joints until he thought to work his hands into the pigs' hot wastes, then smeared some onto his skin. The pigs grunted around him and intelligently snuffled at his body with their pink and tender noses, and Ainslie thought, *You are not me but I am you,* and Ainslie Classen got through the night without shame or injury.

Whereas a Hartington woman took two steps out her door and disappeared until the snow sank away in April and raised her body up from her garden patch.

An Omaha cigar maker got off the Leavenworth Street trolley that night, fifty yards from his own home and five yards from another's. The completeness of the blizzard so puzzled him that the cigar maker tramped up and down the block more than twenty times and then slept against a lamppost and died.

A cattle inspector froze to death getting up on his quarter horse. The next morning he was still tilting the saddle with his upright weight, one cowboy boot just inside the iced stirrup, one bear-paw mitten over the horn and reins. His quarter horse apparently kept waiting for him to complete his mount, and then the quarter horse died too.

A Chicago boy visiting his brother for the holidays was

going to a neighbor's farm to borrow a scoop shovel when the night train of blizzard raged in and overwhelmed him. His tracks showed the boy mistakenly slanted past the sod house he'd just come from, and then tilted forward with perhaps the vain hope of running into some shop or shed or railway depot. His body was found four days later and twenty-seven miles from home.

A forty-year-old wife sought out her husband in the open range land near O'Neill and days later was found standing up in her muskrat coat and black bandanna, her scarf-wrapped hands tightly clenching the top strand of rabbit wire that was keeping her upright, her blue eyes still open but cloudily bottled by a half inch of ice, her jaw unhinged as though she'd died yelling out a name.

The one a.m. report from the Chief Signal Officer in Washington, D.C., had said Kansas and Nebraska could expect "fair weather, followed by snow, brisk to high southerly winds gradually diminishing in force, becoming westerly and warmer, followed by colder."

Sin Thomas undertook the job of taking Emily Flint home from their Holt County schoolhouse just before noon. Sin's age was sixteen, and Emily was not only six years younger but also practically kin to him, since her stepfather was Sin's older brother. Sin took the girl's hand and they haltingly tilted against the uprighting gale on their walk to a dark horse, gray-maned and gray-tailed with ice. Sin cracked the reins loose of the crowbar tie-up and helped Emily up onto his horse, jumping up onto the croup from a soapbox and clinging the girl to him as though she were groceries he couldn't let spill.

Everything she knew was no longer there. She was in a book without descriptions. She could put her hand out and her hand would disappear. Although Sin knew the general direction to Emily's house, the geography was so duned and drunk with snow that Sin gave up trying to nudge his horse one way or another and permitted its slight adjustments away from the wind. Hours passed and the horse strayed southeast into Wheeler County, and then in misery and pneumonia it stopped, planting its overworked legs like four parts of an argument and slinging its head away from Sin's yanks and then hanging its nose in anguish. Emily hopped down into the snow and held on to the boy's coat pocket as Sin uncinched the saddle and jerked off a green horse blanket and slapped it against his iron leggings in order to crack the ice from it. And then Sin scooped out a deep nook in a snow slope that was as high and steep as the roof of a New Hampshire house. Emily tightly wrapped herself in the green horse blanket and slumped inside the nook in the snow, and the boy crept on top of her and stayed like that, trying not to press into her.

Emily would never say what was said or was cautiously not said that night. She may have been hysterical. In spite of the fact that Emily was out of the wind, she later said that the January night's temperature was like wire-cutting pliers that snipped at her ears and toes and fingertips until the horrible pain became only a nettling and then a kind of sleep and her feet seemed as dead as her shoes. Emily wept, but her tears froze cold as penny nails and her upper lip seemed candlewaxed by her nose and she couldn't stop herself from feeling the difference in the body on top of her. She thought Sin Thomas was responsible, that the night suited his secret purpose, and she so complained of the bitter cold that Sin finally took off his Newmarket overcoat and tailored it around the girl; but sixty years later, when Emily wrote her own account of the ordeal, she forgot to say anything about him giving her his overcoat and only said in an ordinary way that they spent the night inside a snowdrift and that "by morning the storm had subsided."

With daybreak Sin told Emily to stay there and, with or without his Newmarket overcoat, the boy walked away with the forlorn hope of chancing upon his horse. Winds were still high, the temperature was thirty-five degrees below zero, and the snow was deep enough that Sin pulled lopsidedly with every step and then toppled over just a few yards away. And then it was impossible for him to get to his knees, and Sin only sank deeper when he attempted to swim up into the high wave of snow hanging over him. Sin told himself that he would try again to get out, but first he'd build up his strength by napping for just a little while. He arranged his body in the snow gully so that the sunlight angled onto it, and then Sin Thomas gave in to sleep and within twenty minutes died.

His body was discovered at noon by a Wheeler County search party, and shortly after that they came upon Emily. She was carried to a nearby house where she slumped in a kitchen chair while girls her own age dipped Emily's hands and feet into pans of ice water. She could look up over a windowsill and see Sin Thomas's body standing upright on the porch, his hands woodenly crossed at his chest, so Emily kept her brown eyes on the pinewood floor and slept that night with jars of hot water against her skin. She could not walk for two months. Even scissoring tired her hands. She took a cashier's job with the Nebraska Farm Implements Company and kept it for forty-five years, staying all her life in Holt County. She died in a wheelchair on a hospital porch in the month of April. She was wearing a glamorous sable coat. She never married.

The T. E. D. Schusters' only child was a seven-year-old boy named Cleo who rode his Shetland pony to the Westpoint school that day and had not shown up on the doorstep by two p.m., when Mr. Schuster went down into the root cellar, dumped purple sugar beets onto the earthen floor, and upended the bushel basket over his head as he slung himself against the onslaught in his second try for Westpoint. Hours later Mrs. Schuster was tapping powdered salt onto the night candles in order to preserve the wax when the door abruptly blew open and Mr. Schuster stood there without Cleo and utterly white and petrified with cold. She warmed him up with okra soup and tenderly wrapped his frozen feet and hands in strips of gauze that she'd dipped in kerosene, and they were sitting on milking stools by a red-hot stove, their ankles just touching, only the usual sentiments being expressed, when they heard a clopping on the wooden stoop and looked out to see the dark Shetland pony turned gray and shaggy-bearded with ice, his legs as wobbly as if he'd just been born. Jammed under the saddle skirt was a damp, rolled-up note from the Scottish schoolteacher that said, Cleo is safe. The Schusters invited the pony into the house and bewildered him with praises as Cleo's mother scraped ice from the pony's shag with her own ivory comb, and Cleo's father gave him sugar from the Dresden bowl as steam rose up from the pony's back.

Even at six o'clock that evening, there was no heat in Mathias Aachen's house, and the seven Aachen children were in whatever stockings and clothing they owned as they put their hands on a Hay-burner stove that was no warmer than soap. When a jar of apricots burst open that night and the iced orange syrup did not ooze out, Aachen's wife told the children, You ought now to get under your covers. While the seven were crying and crowding onto their dirty floor mattresses, she rang the green tent cloth along the iron wire dividing the house and slid underneath horse blankets in Mathias Aachen's gray wool trousers and her own gray dress and a ghastly muskrat coat that in hot weather gave birth to insects.

Aachen said, Every one of us will be dying of cold before morning. Freezing here. In Nebraska.

His wife just lay there, saying nothing.

Aachen later said he sat up bodingly until shortly after one a.m., when the house temperature was so exceedingly cold that a gray suede of ice was on the teapot and his pretty girls were whimpering in their sleep. You are not meant to stay here, Aachen thought, and tilted hot candle wax into his right ear and then his left, until he could only hear his body drumming blood. And then Aachen got his Navy Colt and kissed his wife and killed her. And then walked under the green tent cloth and killed his seven children, stopping twice to capture a scuttling boy and stopping once more to reload.

Hattie Benedict was in her Antelope County schoolyard overseeing the noon recess in a black cardigan sweater and gray wool dress when the January blizzard caught her unaware. She had been impatiently watching four girls in flying coats playing Ante I Over by tossing a spindle of chartreuse yarn over the one-room schoolhouse, and then a sharp cold petted her neck and Hattie turned toward the open fields of hoarfrosted scraggle and yellow grass. Just a half mile away was a gray blur of snow underneath a dark sky that was all hurry and calamity, like a nighttime city of sin-black buildings and havoc in the streets. Wind tortured a creekside cottonwood until it cracked apart. A tin water pail rang in a skipping roll to the horse path. One quarter of the tar-paper roof was torn from the schoolhouse and sailed southeast forty feet. And only then did Hattie yell for the older boys with their cigarettes and clay pipes to hurry in from the prairie twenty rods away, and she was hustling a dallying girl inside just as the snowstorm socked into her Antelope County schoolhouse, shipping the building awry off its timber skids so that the southwest side heavily dropped six inches and the oak-plank floor became a slope that Hattie ascended unsteadily while ordering the children to open their *Webster Franklin Fourth Reader* to the Lord's Prayer in verse and to say it aloud. And then Hattie stood by her desk with her pink hands held theatrically to her cheeks as she looked up at the walking noise of bricks being jarred from the chimney and down the roof. Every window view was as white as if butchers' paper had been tacked up. Winds pounded into the windowpanes and dry window putty trickled onto the unpainted sills. Even the slough grass fire in the Hay-burner stove was sucked high into the tin stack pipe so that the soot on it reddened and snapped. Hattie could only stare. Four of the boys were just about Hattie's age, so she didn't say anything when they ignored the reading assignment and earnestly got up from the wooden benches in order to argue *oughts* and *ought nots* in the cloakroom. She heard the girls saying Amen and then she saw Janusz Vasko, who was fifteen years old and had grown up in Nebraska weather, gravely exiting the cloakroom with a cigarette behind one ear and his right hand raised high overhead. Hattie called on him, and Janusz said the older boys agreed that they could get the littler ones home, but only if they went out right away. And before she could even give it thought, Janusz tied his red handkerchief over his nose and mouth and jabbed his orange corduroy trousers inside his antelope boots with a pencil.

Yes, Hattie said, please go, and Janusz got the boys and girls to link themselves together with jump ropes and twine and piano wire, and twelve of Hattie Benedict's pupils walked out into a nothingness that the boys knew from their shoes up and dully worked their way across as though each crooked stump and tilted fence post was a word they could spell in a plain-spoken sentence in a book of practical knowledge. Hours later the children showed up at their homes, aching and crying in raw pain. Each was given cocoa or the green tea of the elder flower and hot bricks were put next to their feet while they napped and newspapers printed their names incorrectly. And then, one by one, the children disappeared from history.

Except for Johan and Alma Lindquist, aged nine and six, who stayed behind in the schoolhouse, owing to the greater distance to their ranch. Hattie opened a week-old Omaha newspaper on her desktop and with caution peeled a spotted yellow apple on it, eating tan slices from her scissor blade as she peered out at children who seemed irritatingly sad and pathetic. She said, You wish you were home.

The Lindquists stared.

Me too, she said. She dropped the apple core onto the newspaper page and watched it ripple with the juice stain. Have you any idea where Pennsylvania is?

East, the boy said. Johan was eating pepper cheese and day-old rye bread from a tin lunch box that sparked with electricity whenever he touched it. And his sister nudged him to show how her yellow hair was beguiled toward her green rubber comb whenever she brought it near.

Hattie was talking in such quick English that she could tell the Lindquists couldn't quite understand it. She kept hearing the snow pinging and pattering against the windowpanes, and the storm howling like clarinets down the stack pipe, but she perceived the increasing cold in the room only when she looked to the Lindquists and saw their Danish sentences grayly blossoming as they spoke. Hattie went into the cloakroom and skidded out the poorhouse box, rummaging from it a Scotch plaid scarf that she wrapped twice around her skull and ears just as a squaw would, and snipping off the fingertips of some red knitted gloves that were only slightly too small. She put them on and then she got into her secondhand coat and Alma whispered to her brother but Hattie said she'd have no whispering, she hated that, she couldn't wait for their kin to show up for them, she had too many responsibilities, and nothing interesting ever happened in the country. Everything was stupid. Everything was work. She didn't even have a girlfriend. She said she'd once been sick for four days, and two by two practically every woman in Neligh mistrustfully visited her rooming house to squint at Hattie and palm her forehead and talk about her symptoms. And then they'd snail out into the hallway and prattle and whisper in the hawk and spit of the German language.

Alma looked at Johan with misunderstanding and terror, and Hattie told them to get out paper and pencils; she was going to say some necessary things and the children were going to write them down. She slowly paced as she constructed a paragraph, one knuckle darkly striping the blackboard, but she couldn't properly express herself. She had forgotten herself so absolutely that she thought forgetting was a yeast in the air; or that the onslaught's only point was to say over and over again that she was next to nothing. Easily bewildered. Easily dismayed. The Lindquists were shying from the crazy woman and concentrating their shame on a nickel pad of Wisconsin paper. And Hattie thought, *You'll give me an ugly name and there will be cartoons and snickering and the older girls will idly slay me with jokes and imitations.*

She explained she was taking them to her rooming house, and she strode purposefully out into the great blizzard as if she were going out to a garden to fetch some strawberries, and Johan dutifully followed, but Alma stayed inside the schoolhouse with her purple scarf up over her mouth and nose and her own dark sandwich of pepper cheese and rye bread clutched to her breast like a prayer book. And then Johan stepped out of the utter whiteness to say Alma had to hurry up, that Miss Benedict was angrily asking him if his sister had forgotten how to use her legs. So Alma stepped out of the one-room schoolhouse, sinking deep in the snow and sloshing ahead in it as she would in a pond until she caught up with Hattie Benedict, who took the Lindquists' hands in her own and walked them into the utter whiteness and night of the afternoon. Seeking to blindly go north to her rooming house, Hattie put her high button shoes in the deep tracks that Janusz and the schoolchildren had made, but she misstepped twice, and that was enough to get her on a screw-tape path over snow humps and hillocks that took her south and west and very nearly into a great wilderness that was like a sea in high gale.

Hattie imagined herself reaching the Elkhorn River and discovering her rooming house standing high and honorable under the sky's insanity. And then she and the Lindquist children would duck over their teaspoons of tomato soup and soda crackers as the town's brooms and scarecrows teetered over them, hooking their green hands on the boy and girl and saying, Tell us about it. She therefore created a heroine's part for herself and tried to keep to it as she floundered through drifts as high as a four-poster bed in a white room of piety and weeping. Hattie pretended gaiety by saying once, See how it swirls! but she saw that the Lindquists were tucking deep inside themselves as they trudged forward and fell and got up again, the wind drawing tears from their squinting eyes, the hard, dry snow hitting their skin like wildly flying pencils. Hours passed as Hattie tipped away from the press of the wind into country that was a puzzle to her, but she kept saying, Just a little farther, until she saw Alma playing Gretel by secretly trailing her right hand along a high wave of snow in order to secretly let go yet another crumb of her rye bread. And then, just ahead of her, she saw some pepper cheese that the girl dropped some time ago. Hissing spindrifts tore away from the snow swells and spiked her face like sharp pins, but then a door seemed to inch ajar and Hattie saw the slight, dark change of a haystack and she cut toward it, announcing that they'd stay there for the night.

She slashed away an access into the haystack and ordered Alma to crawl inside, but the girl hesitated as if she were still thinking of the gingerbread house and the witch's oven, and Hattie acidly whispered, You'll be a dainty mouthful. She meant it as a joke but her green eyes must have seemed crazy, because the little girl was crying when Hattie got inside the haystack next to her, and then Johan was crying, too, and Hattie hugged the Lindquists to her body and tried to shush them with a hymn by Dr. Watts, gently singing, Hush, my dears, lie still and slumber. She couldn't get her feet inside the haystack, but she couldn't feel them anyway just then, and the haystack was making everything else seem right and possible. She talked to the children about hot pastries and taffy and Christmas presents, and that night she made up a story about the horrible storm being a wicked old man whose only thought was to eat them up, but he couldn't find them in the haystack even though he looked and looked. The old man was howling, she said, because he was so hungry.

At daybreak a party of farmers from Neligh rode out on their high plowhorses to the Antelope County schoolhouse in order to get Hattie and the Lindquist children, but the room was empty and the bluetick hound that was with them kept scratching up rye bread until the party walked along behind it on footpaths that wreathed around the schoolyard and into a haystack twenty rods away where the older boys smoked and spit tobacco juice at recess. The Lindquist girl and the boy were killed by the cold, but Hattie Benedict had stayed alive inside the hay, and she wouldn't come out again until the party of men yanked her by the ankles. Even then she kept the girl's body hugged against one side and the boy's body hugged to the other, and when she was put up on one horse, she stared down at them with green eyes that were empty of thought or understanding and inquired if they'd be okay. Yes, one man said. You took good care of them.

Bent Lindquist ripped down his kitchen cupboards and carpentered his own triangular caskets, blacking them with shoe polish, and then swaddled Alma and Johan in black alpaca that was kindly provided by an elder in the Church of Jesus Christ of Latter-Day Saints. And all that night Danish women sat up with the bodies, sopping the Lindquists' skin with vinegar so as to impede putrefaction.

Hattie Benedict woke up in a Lincoln hospital with sweet oil of spermaceti on her hands and lips, and weeks later a Kansas City surgeon amputated her feet with a polished silver hacksaw in the presence of his anatomy class. She was walking again by June, but she was attached to cork-and-iron shoes and she sighed and grunted with every step. Within a year she grew so overweight that she gave up her crutches for a wicker-backed wheelchair and stayed in Antelope County on a pension of forty dollars per month, letting her dark hair grow dirty and leafy, reading one popular romance per day. And yet she complained so much about her helplessness, especially in winter, that the Protestant churches took up a collection and Hattie Benedict was shipped by train to Oakland, California, whence she sent postcards saying she'd married a trolley repairman and she hated Nebraska, hated their horrible weather, hated their petty lives.

* * *

On Friday the thirteenth some pioneers went to the upper stories of their houses to jack up the windows and crawl out onto snow that was like a jeweled ceiling over their properties. Everything was sloped and planed and caped and whitely furbelowed. One man couldn't get over his boyish delight in tramping about on deer-hide snowshoes at the height of his roof gutters, or that his dogwood tree was forgotten but for twigs sticking out of the snow like a skeleton's fingers. His name was Eldad Alderman, and he jabbed a bamboo fishing pole in four likely spots a couple of feet below his snowshoes before the bamboo finally thumped against the plank roof of his chicken coop. He spent two hours spading down to the coop and then squeezed in through the one window in order to walk among the fowl and count up. Half his sixty hens were alive; the other half were still nesting, their orange beaks lying against their white hackles, sitting there like a dress shop's hats, their pure white eggs not yet cold underneath them. In gratitude to those thirty chickens that withstood the ordeal, Eldad gave them Dutch whey and curds and eventually wrote a letter praising their constitutions in the *American Poultry Yard.*

Anna Shevschenko managed to get oxen inside a shelter sturdily constructed of oak scantling and a high stack of barley straw, but the snow powder was so fine and fiercely penetrating that it sifted through and slowly accumulated on the floor. The oxen tamped it down and inchingly rose toward the oak scantling rafters, where they were stopped as the snow flooded up, and by daybreak were overcome and finally asphyxiated. Widow Shevschenko decided then that an old woman could not keep a Nebraska farm alone, and she left for the East in February.

One man lost three hundred Rhode Island Red chickens; another lost two hundred sixty Hereford cattle and sold their hides for two dollars apiece. Hours after the Hubenka boy permitted twenty-one hogs to get out of the snowstorm and join their forty Holsteins in the upper barn, the planked floor in the cattle linter collapsed under the extra weight and the livestock perished. Since even coal picks could no more than chip the earth, the iron-hard bodies were hauled aside until they could be put underground in April, and just about then some Pawnee Indians showed up outside David City. Knowing their manner of living, Mr. Hubenka told them where the carcasses were rotting in the sea wrack of weed tangles and thaw-water jetsam, and the Pawnee rode their ponies onto the property one night and hauled the carrion away.

And there were stories about a Union Pacific train being arrested by snow on a railway siding near Lincoln, and the merchandisers in the smoking car playing euchre, high five, and flinch until sunup; about cowboys staying inside a Hazard bunkhouse for three days and getting bellyaches from eating so many tins of anchovies and saltine crackers; about the Omaha YMCA where shop clerks paged through inspirational pamphlets or played checkers and cribbage or napped in green leather Chesterfield chairs until the great blizzard petered out.

Half a century later, in Atkinson, there was a cranky talker named Bates, who maintained he was the fellow who first thought of attaching the word *blizzard* to the onslaught of high winds and slashing dry snow and ought to be given credit for it. And later, too, a Lincoln woman remembered herself as a little girl peering out through yellowed window paper at a yard and countryside that were as white as the first day of God's creation. And then a great white Brahma bull with street-wide horns trotted up to the house, the night's snow puffing up from his heavy footsteps like soap flakes, gray funnels of air flaring from his nostrils and wisping away in the horrible cold. With a tilt of his head the great bull sought out the hiding girl under a Chesterfield table and, having seen her, sighed and trotted back toward Oklahoma.

Wild turkey were sighted over the next few weeks, their wattled heads and necks just above the snow like dark sticks, some of them petrified that way but others simply waiting for happier times to come. The onslaught also killed prairie dogs, jackrabbits, and crows, and the coyotes that relied upon them for food got so hungry that skulks of them would loiter like juveniles in the yards at night and yearn for scraps and castaways in old songs of agony that were always misunderstood.

Addie Dillingham was seventeen and irresistible that January day of the great blizzard, a beautiful English girl in an hourglass dress and an ankle-length otter-skin coat that was sculpted brazenly to display a womanly bosom and bustle. She had gently agreed to join an upperclassman at the Nebraska School of Medicine on a journey across the green ice of the Missouri River to Iowa, where there was a party at the Masonic Temple in order to celebrate the final linking of Omaha and Council Bluffs. The medical student was Repler Hitchcock of Council Bluffs—a good companion, a Republican, and an Episcopalian—who yearned to practice electro-therapeutics in Cuernavaca, Mexico. He paid for their three-course luncheon at the Paxton Hotel and then the couple strolled down Douglas Street with four hundred other partygoers, who got into cutters and one-horse open sleighs just underneath the iron legs and girders of what would eventually be called the Ak-Sar-Ben Bridge. At a cap-pistol shot the party jerked away from Nebraska and there were champagne toasts and cheers and yahooing, but gradually the party scattered and Addie could only hear the iron shoes of the plowhorse and the racing sleigh hushing across the shaded window glass of river, like those tropical flowers shaped like saucers and cups that slide across the green silk of a pond of their own accord.

At the Masonic Temple there were coconut macaroons and hot syllabub made with cider and brandy, and quadrille dancing on a puncheon floor to songs like the "Butterfly Whirl" and "Cheater Swing" and "The Girl I Left Behind Me." Although the day was getting dark and there was talk about a great snowstorm roistering outside, Addie insisted on staying out on the dance floor until only twenty people remained and the quadrille caller had put away his violin and his sister's cello. Addie smiled and said, Oh what fun! as Repler tidily helped her into her mother's otter-skin coat and then escorted her out into a grand empire of snow that Addie thought was thrilling. And then, although the world by then was wrathfully meaning everything it said, she walked alone to the railroad depot at Ninth and Broadway so she could take the one-stop train called The Dummy across to Omaha.

Addie sipped hot cocoa as she passed sixty minutes up close to the railroad depot's coal stoker oven and some other partygoers sang of Good King Wenceslaus over a parlor organ. And then an old yardman who was sheeped in snow trudged through the high drifts by the door and announced that no more trains would be going out until morning.

Half the couples stranded there had family in Council Bluffs and decided to stay overnight, but the idea of traipsing back to Repler's house and sleeping in his sister's trundle bed seemed squalid to Addie, and she decided to walk the iron railway trestle across to Omaha.

Addie was a half hour away from the Iowa railway yard and up on the tracks over the great Missouri before she had second thoughts. White hatchings and tracings of snow flew at her horizontally. Wind had rippled snow up against the southern girders so that the high white skin was pleated and patterned like oyster shell. Every creosote tie was tented with snow that angled down into dark troughs that Addie could fit a leg through. Everything else was night sky and mystery, and the world she knew had disappeared. And yet she walked out onto the trestle, teetering over to a catwalk and sidestepping along it in high-button shoes, forty feet above the ice, her left hand taking the yield from one guy wire as her right hand sought out another. Yelling winds were yanking at her, and the iron trestle was swaying enough to tilt her over into nothingness, as though Addie Dillingham were a playground game it was just inventing. Halfway across, her gray tam-o'-shanter was snagged out just far enough into space that she could follow its spider-drop into the night, but she only stared at the great river that was lying there moon-white with snow and intractable. Wishing for her jump.

Years later Addie thought that she got to Nebraska and did not give up and was not overfrightened because she was seventeen and could do no wrong, and accidents and dying seemed a government you could vote against, a mother you could ignore. She said she panicked at one jolt of wind and sank down to her knees up there and briefly touched her forehead to iron that hurt her skin like teeth, but when she got up again, she could see the ink-black stitching of the woods just east of Omaha and the shanties on timber piers just above the Missouri River's jagged stacks of ice. And she grinned as she thought how she would look to a vagrant down there plying his way along a rope in order to assay his trotlines for gar and catfish and then, perhaps, appraising the night as if he'd heard a crazy woman screaming in a faraway hospital room. And she'd be jauntily up there on the iron trestle like a new star you could wish on, and as joyous as the last high notes of "The Girl I Left Behind Me."

Playland

After the agricultural exhibit of 1918, some partners in a real-estate development firm purchased the cattle barns, the gymkhana, the experimental alfalfas and sorghums, the paddocks and pear orchards, and converted one thousand acres into an amusement park called Playland. A landscape architect from Sardinia was persuaded to oversee garden construction, and the newspapers made much of his steamship passage and arrival by train in a December snow, wearing a white suit and boater. Upon arrival he'd said, "It is chilly," a sentence he'd practiced for two hundred miles.

He invented gardens as crammed as flower shops, glades that were like dark green parlors, ponds that gently overlipped themselves so that water sheeted down to another pond, and trickle streams that issued from secret pipes sunk in the crannies of rocks. Goldfish with tails like orange scarves hung in the pools fluttering gill fins or rising for crumbs that children sprinkled down. South American and African birds were freighted to Playland, each so shockingly colored that a perceiver's eyes blinked as from a photographer's flash. They screamed and mimicked and battered down onto ladies' hats or the perch of an index finger, while sly yellow canaries performed tricks of arithmetic with green peas and ivory thimbles. Cats were removed from the premises, dogs had to be leashed, policemen were instructed to whistle as they patrolled "so as not to surprise visitors to the park at moments of intimacy."

The corn pavilion was transformed into trinket shops, two clothing stores, a bank, a bakery where large chocolate-chip cookies were sold while still hot from the oven, and a restaurant that served cottage-fried potatoes with catfish that diners could snag out of a galvanized tank. The carnival galleries were made slightly orange with electric arc lights overhead, as was the miniature golf course with its undulating green carpets—each hole a foreign country represented by a fjord, pagoda, minaret, windmill, pyramid, or the like. The Ferris wheels and merry-go-rounds were turned by diesel truck engines that were framed with small barns and insulated lest they allow more than a grandfatherly noise; paddlewheel craft with bicycle pedals chopped down a slow, meandering river. Operas and starlight concerts were staged from April to October, and the exhibition place was redecorated at great cost for weekend dances at which evening gowns and tuxedos were frequently required. A pretty ice-skating star dedicated the ballroom, cutting the ribbon in a hooded white mink coat that was so long it dragged dance wax onto the burgundy carpet. A newspaper claimed she'd been tipsy, that she'd said, "You got a saloon in this place?" But after a week's controversy an editor determined that the word she'd used was *salon,* and later the entire incident was denied, the reporter was quietly sent away, and the newspaper grandly apologized to the Playland management.

Lovers strolled on the swept brick sidewalks and roamed on resilient lawns that cushioned their shoes like a mattress, and at night they leaned against the cast-iron lampposts, whispering promises and nicely interlocking their fingers. Pebbled roads led to nooks where couples were roomed by exotic plants and resplendent flowers whose scent was considered an aphrodisiac, so that placards suggesting temperance and restraint were tamped into the pansy beds.

The park speedily rose to preeminence as the one place in America for outings, holidays, company picnics, second honeymoons, but its reputation wasn't truly international until the creation of the giant swimming pool.

Construction took fourteen months. Horse stables were converted to cabanas, steam-powered earth movers sloped the racetrack into a saucer, the shallows and beach were paved, and over twenty thousand railroad cars of Caribbean sand were hauled in on a spur. The pool was nearly one mile long, more than half of that in width, and thirty-six feet deep in its center, where the water was still so pellucid that a swimmer could see a nickel wink sunlight from the bottom. Twelve thousand gallons of water evaporated each summer day and were replaced by six artesian wells feeding six green fountains on which schooling brass fish spouted water from open mouths as they seemed to flop and spawn from a roiling upheaval.

And the beach was a marvel. The sand was as fine as that in hotel ashtrays, so white that lifeguards sometimes became snow-blind, and so deep near the soda-pop stands that a magician could be buried in it standing up, and it took precious minutes for a crew with spades to pull him out when his stunt failed—he gasped, "A roaring noise. A furnace. Suffocation." Gymnasts exercised on silver rings and pommel horses and chalked parallel bars, volleyball tournaments were played there, oiled muscle men pumped dumbbells and posed, and in August girls in saucy bathing suits and high heels walked a gangway to compete for the Miss Playland title. Admission prices increased each season, and yet two million people and more pushed through the turnstiles at Playland during the summers. Playland was considered pleasing and inexpensive entertainment, it represented gracious fellowship, polite surprise, good cheer. The Depression never hurt Playland, cold weather only increased candy sales, rains never seemed to persist for long, and even the periodic scares—typhoid in the water, poisonous snakes in sand burrows, piranha near the diving platform—couldn't shrink the crowds. Nothing closed Playland, not even the war.

Soldiers on furlough or medical release were allowed free entrance, and at USO stations on the beach, happy women volunteers dispensed potato chips and hot dogs on paper plates, sodas without ice, and pink towels just large enough to scrunch up on near the water. Young men would queue up next to the spiked iron fence at six o'clock in the morning when a camp bus dropped them off, and they'd lounge and smoke and squat on the sidewalk reading newspapers, perhaps whistling at pretty girls as the streetcars screeched past. As the golden gates whirred open, the GIs collided and jostled through, a sailor slapped a petty officer's cap off, and little children raced to the teeter-totters and swings as Playland's nursemaids applauded their speed.

The precise date was never recorded, but one morning a corporal named Gordon limped out of the bathhouse and was astonished to see an enormous pelican on the prow of the lifeguard's rowboat. The pelican's eyes were blue beads, and she swung her considerable beak to the right and left to regard Gordon and blink, then she flapped down to the beach and waddled toward him, her wings amorously fanning out to a span of ten feet or more as she struck herself thumpingly on the breast with her beak until a spot of red blood appeared on her feathers. The corporal retreated to the bathhouse door and flung sand at the bird and said, "Shoo!" and the pelican seemed to resign herself and lurched up into eastward flight, her wings loudly swooping the air with a noise like a broom socking dust from a rug on a clothesline.

More guests drifted out of the bathhouse. Children carried tin shovels and sand pails. Married women with bare legs and terry-cloth jackets walked in pairs to the shade trees, sharing the heft of a picnic basket's straw handle. Pregnant women sat on benches in cotton print dresses. Girls emerged into the sun, giggling about silly nothings, their young breasts in the squeeze of crossed arms. On gardened terraces rich people were oiled and massaged by stocky women who spoke no English. Dark waiters in pink jackets carried iced highballs out on trays. A perplexed man in an ascot and navy-blue blazer stood near the overflowing food carts with a dark cigarette, staring down at the pool. Red and yellow hot-air balloons rose up from the apricot orchard and carried in the wind. A rocket ship with zigzag fins and sparking runners and a science-fiction arsenal screamed by on an elevated rail. Children were at the portholes, their noses squashed to the window glass like snails.

A girl of seventeen sat on the beach with her chin in her hands, looking at the mall. Her name was Bijou. A rubber pillow was bunched under her chest and it made her feel romantic. She watched as her boyfriend, the corporal named Gordon, limped barefoot away from a USO stand in khaki pants belted high at his ribs, a pink towel yoking his neck, a cane in his left hand. He dropped his towel next to Bijou's and squared it with his cane's rubber tip. He huffed as he sat and scratched at the knee of his pants. He'd been a messenger between commanders' posts in Africa and rode a camouflaged motorcycle. A mine explosion ruined his walk. Bijou wondered if she was still in love with him. She guessed that she was.

Bijou knelt on her beach blanket and dribbled baby oil onto her thighs. Her white swimming suit was pleated at her breasts but scooped revealingly under her shoulder blades so that pale men wading near her had paused to memorize her prettiness, and a man with a battleship tattoo on his arm had sloshed up onto the hot sand and sucked in his stomach. But Gordon glowered and flicked his cane in a dispatching manner and the man walked over to a girls' badminton game and those in the water lurched on.

"My nose itches," Bijou said. "That means someone's going to visit me, doesn't it?"

"After that pelican I don't need any more surprises," Gordon replied, and then he saw an impressive shadow fluctuate along the sand, and he looked heavenward to see an airplane dip its wings and turn, then lower its flaps and slowly descend from the west, just over a splashing fountain. His eyes smarted from the silver glare of the steel and porthole windows. The airplane slapped down in a sudden spray of water, wakes rolling outward from canoe floats as it cut back its engines and swung around. The propellers chopped and then idled, and a door flapped open as a skinny young man in a pink double-breasted suit stepped down to a rocking lifeguard's boat.

"Must be some bigwig," said Gordon.

The airplane taxied around, and Bijou could see the pilot check the steering and magnetos and instruments, then plunge the throttle forward, ski across the water, and wobble off. The rowboat with the airplane's passenger rode up on the beach and retreated some before it was hauled up by a gang of boys. The man in the pink suit slipped a dollar to a lifeguard and hopped onto the sand, sinking to his ankles. As he walked toward Bijou he removed a pack of cigarettes and a lighter from his shirt pocket. His pants were wide and pleated and he'd cocked a white Panama hat on his head. He laid a cigarette on his lip and grinned at Bijou, and arrested his stride when he was over her.

"Don't you recognize your cousin?"

She shaded her eyes. "Frankie?"

He clinked his cigarette lighter closed and smiled as smoke issued from his nose. "I wanted to see how little Bijou turned out, how this and that developed."

"I couldn't be more surprised!"

He'd ignored the corporal, so Gordon got up, brushing sand from his khakis, and introduced himself. "My name's Gordon. Bijou's boyfriend."

"Charmed," Frankie said. He removed his hat and wiped his brow with a handkerchief. His wavy hair was black and fragrantly oiled and he had a mustache like William Powell's. He had been a radio actor in New York. He asked if they served drinks on the beach, and Gordon offered to fetch him something, slogging off to a soda-pop stand.

"Sweet guy," Frankie said. "What's he got, polio or something?"

"He was wounded in the war."

"The dope," Frankie said. He unlaced his white shoes and unsnapped his silk socks from calf garters and removed them. He slumped down on Gordon's towel, unbuttoning his coat.

"You're so handsome, Frankie!"

"Ya think so?"

"I can't get over it. How'd you find me at Playland?"

"You're not that hard to pick out," Frankie said, and he gave his cousin the once-over. "You look like Betty Grable in that suit."

"You don't think it's too immodest?"

"You're a feast for the eyes."

The corporal returned with an orange soda and a straw. Frankie accepted it without thanks and dug in his pocket for a folded dollar bill. "Here, here's a simoleon for your trouble."

"Nah," Gordon said. "You can get the next round."

Frankie sighed as if bored and poked the dollar bill into the sand near Gordon's bare left foot. He leaned back on his elbows and winked at someone in the pool. "Somebody wants you, Sarge."

"Say again?"

"Two dames in a boat."

A rowboat had scraped bottom, and two adolescent girls with jammy lipstick, Gordon's sister and her girlfriend, motioned for him to come over. Gordon waded to where the water was warm at his calves and climbed darkly up his pant legs. "What're you doing, Sis?"

"Having fun. Where's Bijou?"

"On the beach, Goofy."

His sister strained to see around him. "*Where?*"

He turned. Bijou and Frankie had disappeared.

Frankie strolled the hot white sand with his cousin and sipped orange soda through the straw. Hecklers repeatedly whistled at Bijou and Frankie winked at them. "Hear that? You're the berries, kid. You're driving these wiseacres off their nut."

"Oh, those wolves do that to any female."

"Baloney!" He was about to make a statement but became cautious and revised it. "What am I, nine years older than you?"

"I think so," Bijou said.

"And what about GI Joe?"

Bijou glanced over her shoulder and saw her boyfriend hunting someone on the beach. Gordon squinted at her and she waved, but he seemed to look past her. "He's twenty-one," she said.

"Four years older. What's he doing with a kid like you for his bim?"

"He's mad about me, Stupid."

Frankie snickered. He crossed his ankles and settled down in the bathhouse shade. Bijou sat next to him. Frankie pushed his cigarette down in the sand and lit another, clinking his lighter closed. "Do you and Gordo smooch?"

Bijou prodded sand from between her toes. "Occasionally."

"How shall I put it? You still Daddy's little girl?"

"You're making me uncomfortable, Frankie."

"Nah, I'm just giving you the needle."

The corporal was confused. His nose and shoulders were sunburned and his legs ached and Bijou and Frankie had flat out evaporated. His sister and her girlfriend stroked the rowboat ahead and Gordon sat on the rim board near a forward oarlock, scouting the immeasurable Playland beach. Soon his sister complained that she was tired and bored and blistered, and Gordon said, "All right already. Cripes—don't think about me. Do what you want to do."

After a while Frankie clammed up and then decided he wanted a little exercise and removed his tie and pink coat as he walked past the USO stand to the gym equipment. He performed two pull-ups on the chalked high bar, biting his cigarette, then amused a nurse in the first-aid station with his impressions of Peter Lorre, Ronald Colman, Lionel Barrymore.

"I love hearing men talk," the nurse said. "That's what I miss most."

"Maybe I could close this door," Frankie said.

"You can't kiss me, if that's what you're thinking. I'm not fast."

"Maybe I should amscray, then."

"No!" the nurse said, and shocked herself with her insistence. "Oh, shoot." She turned her back and walked to the sickbed. "Go ahead and close the door."

Anchored in Playland's twenty-foot waters were five diving platforms fixed as star points radiating out from a giant red diving tower with swooping steel buttresses and three levels, the topmost being a crow's nest that was flagged with snapping red pennants. It reached one hundred feet above the surface and was closed off except for the professionals paid to somersault dangerously from the perch at two and four in the afternoon, nine o'clock at night.

And there Gordon had his sister and her girlfriend row him after he'd wearied of looking for Bijou. The boat banged into a steel brace, and the corporal left his cane and walked off the board seat to a ladder slat. He ascended to the first elevation and saw only shivering children who leaned to see that the bottom was unpopulated, then worked up their courage and leapt, shouting paratrooper jump calls. At the second elevation was a short man with gray hair and a very brief suit and skin nearly chocolate brown. The man paused at the edge, adjusting his toes, and then jackknifed off, and Gordon bent out to see him veer into the water sixty feet down. Gordon wanted to recoup, to do something masculine and reckless and death-defying. He yelled to the platform below him, "Anybody down there?" and there was no answer. Then he saw a woman in a white bathing suit like Bijou's underwater near the tower. Her blond hair eddied as she tarried there below the surface. Gordon grinned.

His sister and her girlfriend were spellbound. They saw Gordon carefully roll up his pant cuffs and yank his belt tight through his brass buckle clasp. They saw him simply walk off the second level into a careening drop that lasted almost two seconds. A geyser shot up twenty feet when he smacked the water, then the surface ironed out and his sister worried; finally he burst up near the boat.

"Something's down there!"

"What is?"

"Don't know!" Gordon swam over, wincing with pain, and when he gripped the boat, blood braided down his fist.

Bijou strapped on a white rubber bathing cap and pushed her hair under it as she tiptoed on the hot sand. She splashed water onto her arms and chest, and then crouched into the pool and swam overhand toward a rocking diving platform. It floated on groaning red drums that lifted and smacked down and lifted again as boys dived from the boards. Bijou climbed a ladder and dangled her legs from a diving platform carpeted with drenched rope. She removed her cap, tossed her blond hair, ignored the oglers who hung near the ladder. Her breasts ached and she wished Gordon could somehow rub them without making her crazy.

The diving platform had sloped because a crowd took up a corner, staring toward the diving tower. Bijou saw that the ferry had stopped and that its passengers had gathered at the rail under the canopy, gaping in the same direction. Four lifeguards hung on a rowboat, struggling with something, as a policeman with a gaff hook stood in the boat and Gordon clinched the anchor lock with a bandaged right hand. Gordon! Two swimmers disappeared under water, and the policeman hooked the gaff and they heaved up a black snapping turtle as large as a manhole cover and so heavy that the gaff bowed like a fishing rod. The turtle's thorny neck hooked madly about and its beak clicked as it struck at the gaff and its clawed webs snagged at whatever they could, as if they wanted to rake out an eye. Bijou's boyfriend manipulated a canvas mailbag over the turtle's head and nicked it over the turtle's horned shell. The policeman heard a woman shriek, then saw the hubbub and the astonished crowds on the ferry and diving platforms, and he kicked the turtle onto the boat's bottom and said, "Hide it. Hurry up, hide it."

That night the exhibition palace burned so many light bulbs that signs at the gate warned visitors not to linger too close to the marquee or stare at the electrical dazzle without the green cellophane sunglasses available at the ticket booth. Limousines seeped along an asphalt cul-de-sac that was redolent with honeysuckle, violets, and dahlias, and at least forty taxicabs idled against the curb, the drivers hanging elbows out or sitting against their fenders. Gordon stood on a sidewalk imbedded with gold sparkle and laced his unbandaged fingers with Bijou's as Frankie ostentatiously paid for their admission. Then Bijou left for the powder room with her evening gown in a string-tied box, a pair of white pumps in her hand.

Frankie sauntered inside with Gordon, commenting on the sponge of the burgundy lobby carpet, the vast dance floor's uncommon polish, the vapored fragrances shot overhead from jet instruments tucked into the ceiling's scrolled molding. Bijou's two escorts selected a corner cocktail table and listened to the Butch Seaton Orchestra in sleepy, mopey solitude, without criticism or remark. Then Bijou glided down the ballroom stairs in her glamorous white gown, looking like Playland's last and best creation, Playland's finishing touch, and the men rose up like dukes.

Gordon danced with her and Frankie cut in. Frankie murmured at her ear over sodas, and Gordon asked Bijou to accompany him to the dance floor. The three bandied conversations during breaks, then music would start and they'd detach again. Male hands sought Bijou's hands as she sat; songs were solicited for her from the orchestra; Gordon fanned a napkin near her when it warmed.

By ten o'clock the great ballroom was jammed. Young Marines introduced themselves and danced with uneasy strangers, a sergeant danced with a hatcheck girl, some women danced with each other as the Butch Seaton Orchestra played "Undecided," "Boo Hoo," "Tangerine." Bijou stood near the stage, her boyfriend's hand at her back, his thumb independently diddling her zipper as a crooner sang, "I love you, there's nothing to hide. It's better than burning inside. I love you, no use to pretend. There! I've said it again!" Sheet music turned. A man licked his saxophone reed. The crooner retreated from the microphone as woodwinds took over for a measure. A mirrored sunburst globe rotated on the ceiling, wiping light spots across a man's shoulder, a woman's face, a tasseled drape, a chair. The orchestra members wore white tuxedos with red paper roses in their lapels. Gordon's fingers gingered up Bijou's bare back to her neck, where fine blonde hairs had come undone from an ivory barrette. Bijou shivered and then gently swiveled into Gordon, not meaning to dance but moving with him when he did. His shoes nudged hers, his khaki uniform smelled of a spicy after-shave that Bijou regretted, his pressure against her body made her feel secure and loving.

The music stopped and Gordon said, "Let's ditch your cousin."

"How mean!"

"The guy gives me the creeps."

"Still."

Gordon thumped his cane on the floor and weighed his

hankerings. "How about if you kissed me a big sloppy one right on my ear?"

Bijou giggled. "Not *here.*"

"Maybe later, okay?"

Butch Seaton gripped his baton in both hands and bent into a microphone as a woman in a red evening dress with spangles on it like fish scales crossed to the microphone that the crooner was readjusting lower with a wing nut. The orchestra leader suggested, "And now, Audrey, how about Duke Ellington's soulful tune, 'Mood Indigo'?"

Audrey seemed amenable.

Bijou asked, "I wonder where Frankie is."

"Maybe he was mixing with his kind and somebody flushed him away." The corporal's little joke pleased him, and he was near a guffaw when his nose began to bleed. He spattered drops on his bandaged hand and Bijou's wrist and shoe before he could slump, embarrassed, on a chair with a handkerchief pressed to his nostrils. He remarked, "This day is one for the record books, Bijou. This has been a really weird day."

Bijou complained that she was yukky with Gordon's blood, and she slipped off to the powder room. Gordon watched her disappear among the couples on the dance floor, and then Frankie flopped down on a folding chair next to him.

"How's the schnozzola?" Frankie asked. Gordon removed the handkerchief, and Frankie peered like a vaudeville doctor. "Looks dammed up to me." He slapped Gordon's crippled knee. "I hereby declare you in perfect health. Come on, let's drink to it."

Frankie showed him to a gentleman's saloon, and Gordon paid for a rye whiskey and a Coca-Cola with a simoleon that had grains of sand stuck to it. The Playland glassware was, of course, unblemished with water spots.

Frankie said, "I was a radio actor in New York before the war. I'm coming back from a screen test in Hollywood. Another gangster part. That's about all I do: gunsels, crooks, schlemiels."

"No kidding," the corporal said. He rebandaged his right hand and sulked about his miserable afternoon.

Frankie stared at an eighteenth-century painting of a prissy hunter with two spaniels sniffing at his white leggings, a turkey strangled in his fist. "What a jerk, huh? Here I am, horning in on your girl, and I expect chitchat from you."

"Well, don't expect me to be palsy-walsy. I'll shoot the breeze, okay. But I'm not about to be your pal just because you're Bijou's cousin from Hollywood and radio land."

Frankie scrooched forward on his bar stool. "You oughta see things with my eyes. You take Bijou, for instance. She's a dish, a real hot patootie in anybody's book, but she ain't all she wrote, Gordo, not by a long shot. You and Bijou, you come to Playland, you dance to the music, swallow all this phonus-balonus, and you think you've experienced life to the hilt. Well, I got news for you, GI. You haven't even licked the spoon. You don't know what's out there, what's available." Frankie slid off the bar stool and hitched up his pink pleated pants. "You want a clue, you want a little taste of the hot stuff, you call on Cousin Frankie. I gotta go to the can."

Gordon hunched over his Coca-Cola glass and scowled down into the ice, then swiveled to call to Frankie as he left the saloon, but the schlemiel wasn't there.

Gordon was loitering in the burgundy lobby, slapping his garrison cap in his hand, when Bijou came out of the powder room. He asked, "Do you want to see the moon?"

"Where's Frankie?"

"Who cares?"

A great crush of party goers was pushing against the lobby's glass doors, yelling to get in, each wearing green cellophane sunglasses. Gordon and Bijou exited and a couple was admitted; screams rose and then subsided as the big door closed.

The two strolled past a penny arcade, a calliope, a gypsy fortune-teller's tent, a lavender emporium where chimpanzees in toddler clothes roller-skated and shambled. At a booth labeled Delights, Bijou observed a man spin apples in hot caramel and place them on cupcake papers to cool, and she seemed so fascinated that the corporal bought her one. Bijou chewed the candied apple as they ambled past the stopped rocket ship, an empty French café, a darkened wedding chapel. They walked near pools where great frogs croaked on green lily pads that were as large as place mats, and gorgeous flowers like white cereal bowls drifted in slow turns. The couple strolled into gardens of petunias, loblolly, blue iris, philodendrons, black orchids. Exciting perfumes craved attention, petals detached and fluttered down, a white carnation shattered at the brush of Bijou's hem and piled in shreds on the walk, the air hummed and hushed and whined. Cat's-eye marbles layered a path that veered off into gardens with lurid green leaves overhead, and this walk they took with nervous stomachs and the near panic of erotic desire. The moon vanished and the night cooled. Creepers overtook lampposts and curled up over benches; the wind made the weeping willows sigh like a child in sleep. Playland was everywhere they looked, insisting on itself.

Then Gordon and Bijou were boxed in by black foliage. The corporal involved himself with Bijou and they kissed as they heard the orchestra playing the last dance. Bijou shivered and moved to the music and her boyfriend woodenly followed, his cane slung from a belt loop, his bandaged right hand on her hip. Her cheek nuzzled into his shoulder. His shoes scruffed the grass in a two-step. The music was clarinets and trombones and the crooner singing about heartache, but under that, as from a cellar, Bijou could pick out chilling noises, so secret that they could barely be noticed: of flesh ripped from bone, claws scratching madly at wood, the clink of a cigarette lighter.

Bijou felt the corporal bridle and cease dancing, and then start up again. He danced her around slowly until she could see what he'd seen, but Bijou closed her eyes and said, "Forget about him. Pretend he's not there."

The Killers

His name is Rex. He says he was fifteen his very first time, and says his boss flew back in his chair like he'd been hit in the chest with a fence post. Rex says he worked in the basement wash rack until he got his chance, then he slapped the chamois twice across the hood and watched the boss close up. The garage door rang down on chain pulleys, then the boss rode the belt lift up to his office. Rex opened the car door and lay across the transmission hump to jerk the shotgun out from under the springs. He zipped up his cracked leather coat and rode the lift up to the parking lot's office. He punched himself out on the time clock, wrapped the shotgun up in coveralls, and slid it under the bench. His boss, who was Art, had his pants unbelted, unzipped, tucking in his shirt. He said good night. This was 1960.

Rex walked up the hill to the lunchroom. And down by the auditorium, Ron dropped a cigar at his shoe. Ron was the man who got him the job. Rex says the cigar ash blew red across the sidewalk.

At the lunchroom, Rex ate a fried ham on rye. It used to be a trolley, the lunchroom. Green and yellow and too much light. A man at the end of the counter licked egg yolk off his plate. Rex drank milk until the news came on, then paid the cook with two bills and told him thanks for the change. And no tip.

The guy who got him the job was still down the street. He bent over the match in his hand. Cigar smoke sailed up when he lifted his head. Ron gave him the go-ahead.

Rex stood next to the time clock with the shotgun in his hands and the coveralls on his boot tops. The time clock chunked through four minutes, and I guess Rex thought about how some things would stop and some things would just be beginning. He walked to the office in his stocking feet. When he opened the door, Art looked up.

"I thought you were gone," Art said.

Rex swung the shotgun up and dropped it down on the desktop, cracking the glass. He centered the barrel some with his hip. Art grabbed for it quick and then pitched back in a mess while the big noise shook the windows and gray smoke screwed up to the overhead vent. The chair was pushed back three inches. You could see the skid on the tiles. Art sat there like he was worn-out, his glasses cockeyed on his face. Rex turned out the lights. Luckily he saw how his socks picked up the dirt, so he got out a mop and washed the floor, then put on his boots and locked up. He leaned the shotgun next to the drainpipe and walked down the hill, his hands clasped on top of his stocking cap.

Ron dropped the envelope out of his pocket and was gone.

It was in 1940 that Max leaned across the seat and opened the car door. The man at the corner stooped and looked at him, holding his coat flaps together. "You, huh?"

"Get in."

They drove in silence for a while. Al bit a cuticle and looked at his finger. Al got a cigarette out and lit it with the green coil lighter from the dashboard. The smoke rolled up the window glass and out through the opening where it was chopped off by the wind. At a stoplight Al said, "Look at my hands." He held them, shaking, over the dash. "Would you look at that?"

Max said, "To tell you the truth, I'm a little jumpy too."

The man's eyes were glassy. "You know what I've always been scared of ever since I can remember? I was always afraid I'd wet my pants."

Max smiled.

Al looked out the window. "You think it's funny, but it's not."

"I'll let you relieve yourself first. How would that be?"

"That'd be sweet."

They worked in and out of traffic and found a parking place. Al got out and straightened his coat. He pressed his hair in place in the window reflection. Max got out, flattening a gray muffler against his chest, then buttoning his black wool coat. He put his key in the door and turned it. They both wore light-colored homburg hats. Al tied both his shoes on the bumper.

"How far is it?" he asked.

"Three blocks."

They walked in step on the sidewalk. Max held his hat in the wind.

"What are you using?"

"The Smith and Wesson." He put up the collar on his coat. "That okay with you?"

"Oh, that's just swell, Max. You're a real buddy."

Al stopped to light another cigarette. He coughed badly for a long time, leaning with his arms against a building, hacking between his shoes, then wiping his mouth with a handkerchief. Al shoved his hands in his pockets and hunched forward. The cigarette hung from his lip. "Cold, that's all." Smoke steamed over his face. "I feel it in my ticker when I cough."

"You ought to have it looked at," Max said.

"You're a regular funny boy today, aren't ya?"

They turned left at the corner and walked into a lunchroom that used to be a trolley. A bell jingled over their heads. They sat on stools at the counter and ordered coffee and egg-salad sandwiches. They were the only customers.

"Do you remember the Swede?"

Max nodded.

The counterman turned over the sign that read CLOSED, then got out a broom and began sweeping the floor. He swept under their feet as they ate. Max turned on his stool.

"Is there a place where a fella could get a newspaper?"

"There's a booth at the corner," the counterman said.

Max handed him a dollar bill that the counterman put in his shirt pocket. "Which one you want?"

"Make it the *Trib.*"

He rested his broom against the counter.

"Walk slow."

When the counterman was out the door, Al put down his cup of coffee. "He coulda stayed."

"I know."

"I personally like having people around. Afterward they'll begin to imagine things and get you all wrong in their heads."

Max used a toothpick on all of his teeth. Al put two sticks of chewing gum into his mouth. He crumpled up the wrappers.

"You know how it works," Max said. "You get the call and she says do this, do that. What do you say? She got the wrong number? You do what you have to do. Nothing personal about it." He looked at Al's face in the mirror behind the counter. "What am I telling you this for? You know all the rules." Max got off his stool. "You said you wanted to visit the men's room."

They walked to the back of the place, Max following behind. He stood on a chair to switch on a small radio and turn it up loud. Then he went into the gray lavatory where Al was washing his hands and face. He looked at Max in the spotted mirror. Max was pushing down the fingers of his gloves. He asked, "What'd you do, anyway?"

Al shrugged. "I started taking it easy." He dried his hands with his handkerchief. "I burned myself out as a kid. I lost my vitality."

Max opened his coat. "Do you want to sit down?"

The man sat down under the sink.

Max crouched close, reaching into his shoulder holster. "Waiting's the worst of it. You don't have to do that now." He felt for the heartbeat under Al's shirt, and Al watched him press the Smith and Wesson's muzzle there. Max fired once and the body jerked dead. The arms and legs started jiggling. They were still doing that when Max walked out and closed the men's room door.

He's short, for one thing, so the cuffs on his jeans are rolled up big and he folds a manila paper up four times to put in the heels of his boots. He chews gum instead of brushing his teeth like he should, and pulls his belt so tight that there're tucks and pleats everywhere. He washes his hair with hard yellow soap, then it's rose oil or Vitalis, and he combs it sometimes three or four times before he gets it right. He keeps aspirin in his locker. He says he falls asleep each night with a washrag on his forehead. He punched a tattoo in himself with a ballpoint pen, but it's only a blue star on his wrist and mostly his watch covers it. You can go through school and see his name everywhere: Rex on a wall painted over in beige, Rex on the men's room door, Rex on a desk seat bottom when it's up, Rex Adams stomped out in the snow. He eats oranges at lunch—even the peel!—and gets D's in all his subjects, including music and phys ed. If he comes to sock hops, he just stands there like a squirrel, or like he's waiting for lady's choice. He's always giving me the eye. Especially when I wear dresses. He doesn't have a father or listen to records or play sports. He was the first one in school with a motorcycle, which is chrome and black and waxed and which he saved up for with money from the parking lot. His favorite pastime is collecting magazine pictures, but there's only one taped over his bed; it's from the fifties, from *Life*, about a gangster washed up out of Lake Michigan and swelled up yeasty in his clothes. He says the thing he remembers most is the way the blood seeped into the creases of Art's pants and dripped to the floor like out of a tap when it's not tight. He's got a gun. He's the only Rex in school. He's not cute at all. His shirts all smell like potatoes.

The Swede? That's an old story.

Max had dressed at the hotel window. Leaves rattled in the alley. He crossed his neck with a silk muffler and buttoned a black overcoat tightly across his chest and put on gloves and a derby hat. He met the other man on the street. They both held their hats as they walked.

"I see you got it," Max said.

The man, whose name was Al, said nothing but kept one hand in his pocket.

"Good," Max said.

This was many years ago. This was 1926.

They sat at the counter of Henry's lunchroom facing the mirror. A streetlight came on outside the window. There was a counterman and a black cook and a kid in a cracked leather jacket and cap at the far end of the bar. He had been talking with the counterman when they came in.

Max read the menu and ordered pork tenderloin, but they

weren't serving that until six. They were serving sandwiches. He ordered chicken croquettes but that was dinner too.

"I'll take ham and eggs," Al said.

"Give me bacon and eggs," said Max.

They ate with their gloves on, then Al got down from his stool and took the cook and the boy back to the kitchen and tied them up with towels. Max stared in the mirror that ran along the back of the counter. Al used a catsup bottle to prop open the slit that dishes passed through into the kitchen.

"Listen, bright boy," Al said to the kid. "Stand a little further along the bar."

Then he said, "You move a little to the left, Max."

For a while Max talked about the Swede. He said they were killing him for a friend.

At six-fifteen a streetcar motorman came in, but he went on up the street. Somebody else came in, and the counterman made him a ham and egg sandwich and wrapped it up in oiled paper.

"He can cook and everything," Max said. "You'd make some girl a nice wife."

Max watched the clock. At seven-ten, when the Swede still hadn't shown, Max got off his stool. Al came out from the kitchen hiding the shotgun under his coat.

"So long, bright boy," Al said to the counterman. "You got a lot of luck."

"That's the truth," Max said. "You ought to play the races."

They went out the door and crossed the street.

"That was sloppy," Al said.

"What about where he lives?"

"I don't know this town from apples."

They sat down on the stoop of a white frame house. Inside,

a man and woman were leaning toward a crystal radio. There were doilies on their chairs, and the man slapped his knee when he laughed. Part of a newspaper blew past Max's shoes. He snatched it and opened it up. Al nudged him when the kid in the leather jacket came out of Henry's. They followed the kid up beside the car tracks, turned at the arc light down a side street, and stood in the yard across from Hirsch's rooming house. The kid pushed the bell and a woman let him in.

"The Swede'll come out looking for us," Al said.

"No he won't," Max said. "He'll just sit there and stew."

Al stared across at the second-story window.

After a while the downstairs door opened again and the woman said good night. The kid walked up the dark street to the corner under the arc lights, and then along the car tracks to Henry's lunchroom.

The two men crossed over to the rooming-house yard. Al stepped over a low fence and went around the back. Max walked up the two steps and opened the door. He stood in the hallway and listened and then he climbed a flight of stairs. He softly walked back to the end of a corridor. Al came up the rear stairs from the kitchen. He unbuttoned his coat and cradled the shotgun.

Max knocked on the door but there wasn't an answer.

He turned the handle and pushed the door with his toe. They walked in and closed the door behind them. The Swede was lying on a bed with all his clothes on, just staring at the wall. He used to be a prizefighter and was too long for the bed. He turned to look at them and Al fired.

Rex got the call on a Thursday. His mom was just home from work at the grocery store and he was in his T-shirt and jeans eating a TV dinner and reading a newspaper spread over the ottoman and not paying me any attention. His mom called him to the phone, said it was some man. Ron, it must've been. He put his finger in his ear and turned with the phone, but he still had to ask the guy to repeat this and that. Rex went ahead and jotted everything down on the calendar from church, then tore off the month and folded it up to fit in his leather-braid wallet. Then he sat down on the couch and belched, he's so uncouth. He looked at his TV dinner with the crumb custard still in the dish. Then he got up to run the sink faucet over it and stuff the tray down in the trash. His mom was cooking at the electric range when he was in there. She moved the teakettle onto another coil and dried her hands on her apron and turned around, kind of smiling. He swung his hand back like he was going to slap her, and she screamed and hid under her arms. When he didn't hit her and just grinned instead, she walked right out of the kitchen, heavy on her heels. She was careful around him the majority of the time. You couldn't help but notice.

So Max was an old man now, with a trimmed white beard and brown eyes and size eleven shoes and trouble sleeping nights. He combed his thin hair forward to hide his bald spot. His face was baked red from the sun, his shirts were open at the collar, and he could no longer drink wine. When he last met the man in the black suit, they talked about quail hunting and heavyweight boxing and fishing for marlin off the Keys. Then the man passed a paper to Max, which he signed with a strong cross to the X and a period at the end of his name. They sent a check twice a year. As he stood up he said, "Let me defend the title against all the good young new ones."

He woke early to stand at his easel and paint still lifes, like Cézanne's. They gave him a lot of trouble. The colors were never right. He stacked them in a closet when they were dry. At noon he left the room and walked the city streets or shopped for his evening meal. Or he would sit in the park with a stale loaf of bread and tear up pieces for the pigeons. At night he sat in the stuffed purple chair and listened to German music. Or he wore his reading glasses and slowly turned the pages of art books about Degas or Braque or Picasso.

But windows he'd closed were opened. Books he'd left open were closed. And he sat in the back of a bus and saw a runty kid on a black motorcycle changing lanes, spurting and braking in traffic. He wore goggles and big-cuffed jeans. The kid saw him staring and gave him the finger. Max read his newspaper.

Then Max saw him again at dinner in the lunchroom downstairs. Max ordered the meat loaf special, and the kid walked his machine to the curb. He sat on it, looking at a map. Every now and then he'd wipe his nose on his sleeve.

The coffee was cold. Max told the waitress and she filled a new cup.

"And give me a piece of whatever pie you've got."

"We've got apple and banana cream."

"Whatever's freshest."

She brought him banana cream.

"That your boyfriend out there?"

"Where?"

He pointed.

"Never seen him before."

"He seems to be waiting for somebody."

"He's reading a map. Maybe he's lost."

"Yeah. And maybe he's waiting for somebody."

He wiped his face with a napkin and threw it down. Then he pulled up his pants and went outside.

"Hey!"

The kid was looking at the letters along the right, then the numbers across the top. He tried to put the two lines together.

"Hey, bright boy. You looking for me?"

"What?"

"Do you want me?"

He squirmed in his seat. "No."

Max slapped the map from his hands. It fluttered, then folded in the wind and was blown against a tire.

Max grinned and took a step forward, making fists. The kid hopped off the cycle and into the street. Max put his shoe on the gas tank and pushed. The cycle crashed to the pavement. The back wheel spun free.

The old man was about to tear some wires loose when the kid spit at him. Max straightened slowly and the kid spit again. Max took a few steps back, frowning at the spot on his pant leg, stumbling off-balance, and the kid climbed over the cycle, hacking and working his cheeks. Then he spit again, and it struck Max on the cheek.

The old man backed against the building and took out his handkerchief. "Get outa here, huh? Just leave." He slowly sank to the sidewalk and mopped his face. The kid picked up his cycle.

"That's a dirty, filthy thing to do to anybody," Max said.

The kid started his cycle, then smiled and said, "Oh, you're gonna be easy."

Rex poked a jar of turpentine and it smashed to smithereens on the floor. Then he went and ran his arm recklessly along the top of a chest of drawers and everything—hairbrush, scissors, aerosol cans—spilled to the floor in a racket. There was also a mug of pencils and brushes on a drawing table and he shook them out like pickup sticks. He ripped the sheets off the bed and wadded them up. And he dumped out all the drawers.

We came back at dark and saw the roomer in just his undershirt and slacks, wiping the turpentine up with a paper towel. He was big and had a white beard and he used to be good-looking, you could tell. He looked like he might've been a prizefighter or something.

"There was a guy looking for you," Rex says.

Max was gathering the pencils and brushes and tapping them together. He didn't even notice me there.

"He looked pretty dangerous," Rex says.

Max just dropped pieces of glass in a trash can. They clanged on the tin. He struggled to his feet like a workingman with a chunk of pavement in his hands. He looked for just a second at Rex, then he went to the chest of drawers and began picking up clothes.

The kid sat down at the lunchroom counter and unzipped his cracked leather coat. From the other end of the counter Max watched him. He had been talking to the waitress when the door opened. The waitress gave the kid water and a menu. The kid rubbed his knees with his hands as he read. He said, "I'll have a roast pork tenderloin with applesauce and mashed potatoes."

"Is that on the menu?"

"I've changed my mind," the kid said. "Give me chicken croquettes with green peas and cream sauce and mashed potatoes."

The waitress didn't know what to say.

The kid smiled, and then he stopped smiling. He flicked the menu away. "Just give me ham and eggs."

She wrote on her order pad. "How do you want your eggs?"

"Scrambled."

alternatives

The waitress spoke through the wicket to the cook. The kid put his chin in his hand. He turned his water glass.

Max stared as he drank from his coffee cup and set the cup down in the saucer. The kid jerked his head.

"What are *you* looking at?"

Max put a quarter next to his cup. "Nothing."

Max went to the coat tree. He pulled off a mackinaw jacket and buttoned it on. The kid was swiveled around on his stool. "The hell. You were looking at *me.*"

The waitress had gone through the swinging door in the kitchen. Max blew his nose in a handkerchief. He smiled at the kid. "You're not *half* of what I was."

The kid smiled and leaned back on the counter. "But I'm what's around these days."

It will happen this way:

He'll kick at the door and it will fly open, banging against the wall. Max will be at his easel. He'll try to stand. The kid will hold his gun out and fire. Max will slump off his stool. He'll spill his paints. He'll slam to the floor.

Or Max will open the door and the kid will be to his left. He'll ram the pistol in Max's ear. He'll hold his arm out straight and fire twice.

Or he'll rap three times on the door. When it opens, he'll push his shotgun under Max's nose. Max will stumble back, then sit slowly on the bed where he'll hold his head in his hands. The kid will close the door softly behind him. Max will say, "What are you waiting for?" and the kid will ask, "Where do you want it?" Max will look up, and the kid's gun will buck and the old man will grab his eyes.

Or the kid will let the pistol hang down by his thigh. He'll knock on the door. Max will answer. The kid will step inside, shoving the old man. The pistol will grate against Max's belt buckle until he's backed to the striped bedroom wall. The kid will fire three times, burning the brown flannel shirt. Smoke will crawl up over the collar. The old man will slide to the floor, smearing red on the wall behind him.

Or the door will open a crack. Max will peer out. The kid will shoot, throwing him to the floor. The kid will walk into the room. Max will crawl to a chair, holding his side. He'll sit there in khakis and a blue shirt going black with the blood. He'll say, "I think I'm gonna puke." The kid will say, "Go ahead." He'll say, "I gotta go to the bathroom." He'll pull himself there with the bedposts. Water will run in the sink. He'll come out with a gun. But the kid will fire, and Max's arm will jerk back, his pistol flying. He'll spin and smack his face against a table in his fall.

Or Max will jiggle his keys in one hand while the other clamps groceries tight to his buttoned gray sweater. He'll open the door. The kid will be sitting there in the purple chair by the brushes with a shotgun laid over his legs. The old man will lean against the doorjamb. The groceries will fall. The kid will fire both barrels at the old man's face, hurling him back across the hall. Apples will roll off the rug.

Rex took a wad of rags from a barrel in the garage while I sat against his mom's car brushing my hair. He unwrapped a gun and wiped it off with his shirttail. He sat against his motorcycle seat and turned the chamber round and round, hearing every click. Then he got cold without a coat and covered the gun again and crammed it down his pants. He gave me a weird look. He said, "Ready?"

Max tried to sleep but couldn't. He got up and put on a robe, then took a double-barrel shotgun from the closet, and two shells from a box in one of the drawers. He sat in a stuffed chair by his brushes, lowered the gun butt to the floor, and leaned forward until his eyebrows touched metal. Then he tripped both triggers.

Rex was just about to climb the stairs when he heard the shotgun noise. He just stood there sort of blue and disappointed until I took his hand and pulled him away and we walked over to the lunchroom. Ron was there in a booth in the back. He'd had the pork tenderloin. We sat in the booth with him and as usual he told me how pretty I looked. Rex just sulked, he was so disappointed.

"You should be happy," Ron said.

"Do I still get the money?"

Ron nodded. He was grinning around a cigar. He pushed an envelope across the table.

Rex just looked at it. "Then I guess I *am* happy."

"You should be."

Rex stuffed the envelope inside his coat pocket. Everybody was quiet until I spoke up and said, "I just can't stand to think about him waiting in the room and knowing he's going to get it. It's too damned awful."

Rex looked at me strangely. Ron knocked the ash off his cigar. "Well," he said, "you better not think about it."

His Dog

This was when he first saw her. This was the job where he picked up four hundred dollars. He lifted the collar on his coat and stared into the window reflection of a liquor store across the street and of a fat man in a white shirt turning out the lights in the beer coolers.

The man in the street looked down. The window was the front of a pet shop. In a wicker basket puppies nuzzled and climbed one another in sleep. One of them was loose, prowling. The man tapped the glass with his finger and her ears perked. She had blue eyes. He put on a gruesome rubber mask. The puppy backed away, then yapped and jumped at the glass.

Shh! he said, smiling.

He saw the liquor-store owner begin to pull the iron grate across the high windows.

He crossed the street.

$403.45.

In September, in a park, he saw a boy with the same husky straining at a leash. She was much bigger now, almost grown. The boy dawdled and the pup leaned.

Hey, the man whispered.

The pup turned her head.

Remember?

* * *

He picked bone and gristle and choice bits off the plates in the kitchen of the café. The cook was giving him a weird look. He walked up a dark alley with a plastic bag warm and sticky under his arm. He bumped a garbage can and caught its lid. He peered over a hedge and grinned. He ripped the bag and threw it into the yard and watched the young dog snatch up the meat and jerk it back and drop it to the grass. She carried the bone away and sat there in shadow. He saw her eyes sparkle. She kept staring as he left.

He sat against the chain-link fence. His fingers twisted her fur. Occasionally she licked his chin through the mesh.

It's a crazy way of making a living, he said. Most of the time I just get by. Plus, you're alone all the time.

An autumn wind scattered alley leaves. He lifted the collar of his coat.

He said, I dreamt about you last night.

He said, This is my favorite time of year.

I've been thinking about retiring, he said. How would that be?

He tapped the dollar bills together and wrapped them with rubber bands. He spoke through the rubber mask: And now your change.

The clerk stared at him, his arms at his sides.

Just get out one of those paper sacks and scoop in all the coins.

The clerk raised his hands and suddenly lurched for the gun. There was an explosion. The clerk flew back against a tin rack of cigarettes. He looked down at his bleeding chest. He slowly slid to the floor. He sat.

Goddamn it, the man said. He left the change. Smoke stayed under the light.

* * *

Dew soaked his knees as he unclipped the chain from her collar. She shook her head and shoulders and watched him walk out the gate. He turned and stood there, stooped and unsure. She tilted her head, glanced at the house. He slapped his thigh softly and she dashed to him and knocked him over with her paws.

Hey! he said. Careful.

He cuddled her and struggled to his feet. He turned happy, tottering circles, his eyes brimming. He rubbed his cheek in her fur. You and me, he whispered. You and me.

She was skittish on his bed. He'd roll with the covers and she'd bolt to the floor. He'd drop his arm over her neck and she'd lie there as though her head were caught in a fence. In the morning she balanced on his chest and gazed out the motel window, barking at semi trailer trucks.

As he drove the jeep he scratched his dog's ears. The dog smiled and lifted her nose, so he spidered down the white patch of fur all the way to her chest. Then he looked in the rearview mirror and his hand went to the glove compartment. He put on the rubber mask. He slowed. A family in a station wagon tried to pass him. He looked at them. They dropped back. He cruised for a while and they slipped up on his left again. The children were wide-eyed, the man and woman laughing.

He glowered in his mask. The man floored his car and the children turned in their seats, staring until they vanished over the hill.

He looked at his dog with victory. She panted.

He cranked down the right window and his dog poked her head out. Her nose squirmed in the air.

We're on the lam. Ever hear that word before? It means we're hiding from the cops.

She bit at leaves and branches that slapped against the door. He chuckled. He patted her rump.

I could watch you for hours, you know that?

He set the brake and opened the jeep's door. His dog clambered over him and ran among the pine trees and across a moist, shady yard to the cabin. She sniffed at the door frame, hopped weeds to the back, came out prancing. She wandered to the lake, waded in to her belly, and lapped at the clear water. She walked out heavily and shook, spraying him. He sat on the bank and smoked a cigarette. When his dog came up and licked his face, he petted her so hard her eyes bulged.

He split logs, nailed up shutters, patched the hull of the rowboat, skimmed stones. She stayed with him.

He found an aluminum bowl and poured in brown pellets. He unwrapped a package of meat and sliced raw liver into the meal. He called his dog. When she chewed at her food, the bowl rang.

He pushed himself back from the table and crossed his stocking feet over the arm of the other chair. He lit a cigarette and stared out at the night. Cigarette smoke splashed off the window. He petted her.

You know what?

Her ears perked forward.

This is exactly how I thought it would be.

He pried a tin box, shook an envelope, stuffed it in his coat pocket. He looked through a stamp collection and sighed with puzzlement. He moved on to another room. He dumped a jewelry chest, stirred things with his finger, dropped a pair of earrings and a necklace in his pocket. He smashed the head of a piggy bank, shook it on the bed, picked out the quarters and dimes. The coins clinked in his pocket as he walked down the stairs.

Coming out of the lake house, he saw that his dog, the blue-eyed husky, had a rabbit in her mouth. He buried it and wiped the blood from his hands with a handkerchief. He wouldn't speak to her.

He jerked cupboard doors, banged pans on the stove burners, looked out the cabin window all through the meal. Finally she came to him and rested her head in his lap. He cradled it and played with her ears and tipped her nose up so that her eyes fixed on his.

What's the deal with that rabbit? What's got into you, anyway?

His dog was far ahead of him. There were noises in the distant woods, of tearing leaves and snapping twigs. It sounded like food frying, like talk. He picked up his pace and called to her. He caught his ankle in tangling vines. He shouted her name. The weeds rustled and his dog bounded through, her black fur thorny and snatched with brambles. She circled him and he thumped her side with his hand. He leaned against a tree, rubbed his brow, and looked through the bare upper branches at the sun. He kneaded the muscles of his arms. I'm so afraid I'm going to lose you.

She shook the earrings off every time he clipped them on. The necklace was probably snagged on a stump somewhere.

* * *

He fed the fire and knelt there, staring at his dog. She raised one eyebrow, then the other, and her tail beat against the chair. He broke a piece of kindling and tossed it to a corner. His dog chased the piece, bit it gingerly, flipped it in her mouth. He threw the stick again and his dog ran after it, paws rattling on the floor. They played like that for a while, then he picked up a hot stick from the fire and threw it. A wisp of smoke streamed after it. His dog stood there.

Well, get it.

His dog sat and looked around the room, smiling.

He glared, then stood, feeling his knees.

Good girl.

He sat at the table with his coffee and focused on the calendar tacked to the wall. Then he washed out his cup, put on a coat, and stuffed a gun in his pocket. He stood at the open door and patted his thigh. His dog cocked her head, then slowly walked past him to the jeep.

He followed. We gotta eat, he said.

They drove to a hardware store. He put on his mask and pointed his finger at his dog.

I don't want a sound out of you. I want you to stay put.

His mask quaked when he spoke. His dog's eyes darted and she settled on the floor. He sat there, looking out the windshield, then he opened the door. His dog smoothed her whiskers with her tongue and panted. He scraped his shoes on the wooden steps and walked inside. A bell chimed and he said something.

She smelled the litter basket and the space beneath the seat. She rolled a road flare back and forth, then far under the springs, out of reach.

He opened the door and climbed in, huffing. He angrily turned the ignition and lifted to readjust the gun in his coat pocket. He still had the mask on. He put the jeep in gear and aggressively rubbed his knuckles into her skull.

Hungry? he asked.

That night he crouched by the lake and watched a brief flurry of snowflakes speck the water and dissolve. He trudged back to the cabin and tried the door, but it was locked.

What is this?

He cupped his eyes and peered through the window. His dog lay by the orange fire, repeatedly licking her paw.

He tried the door again and it swung free. His dog looked at him.

The oar tips cut into the water and moved, stirring small whirlpools. The green lake was shiny with calm. He slouched back against the prow and zipped his mackinaw up to the collar. He could only see boat houses, boatless docks, woods of blurry red and gold, and over them a gunmetal sky. It looked as though it might snow again. He was alone on the lake, absolutely. He smiled for a moment and slowly rowed back to the cabin.

He thought, I should've brought a radio.

His dog sat patiently on the sand bank of the lake, her tail wagging, a bird of some sort clamped in her jaws.

What've you got? Huh?

He beached the boat, scraping it on rocks. His boots splashed in the water at the shore. He tamped the anchor into silt. He climbed tiredly to his dog.

Give me that.

He tapped her chin and she let the quail roll into his hand.

He stroked the beak with his thumb and the head waggled. She danced around him and jumped. He held her by the collar, threw the bird to the fringe of the forest, wiped his hands on his pants. He knelt next to his dog and cupped her chin in his hand.

Don't you *ever* do that again!

She tried to pull away. He swatted her nose and she flinched. He was about to speak again when she jerked her head and slinked off. He gripped her collar and yanked her around.

Let's get something straight once and for all. That's the kind of thing I won't tolerate. That's the kind of thing that could ruin whatever we've got going here.

He walked slowly back to the cabin. She wouldn't heel. She crossed in and out of the forest.

You bitch! he shouted.

His boots rasped in gravel. His eyes were warm with tears. Bitch.

By evening she was gone.

He threw wood on the fire. He kicked a chair around. He slumped against the door.

It began to snow in earnest and he went to bed early.

He thought he heard a scratching at the door. He couldn't read the time on his watch. He stayed in bed and listened for the sound. He heard a whimper.

There was a faint pink glow from the fireplace. The door opened heavily with snow packed against it. He stood outside, shivering in his slippers and pajamas. The snow slanted in from the lake and, when the wind died, made the slightest crackle in the trees, like someone way out there was wadding cellophane. He walked around the cabin, sloughing through drifts, and saw nothing.

* * *

The snow jeweled in the sunlight. There were two sets of powdered prints around the cabin. He looked at them, a cigarette in his mouth, rubbing the sleeves of his flannel shirt.

I could've done that, he thought. I could've walked around the place twice. I was sleepy.

Then he sagged a bit and pressed his eyes with his thumb knuckles. He turned to go back inside when he heard a bark.

His dog plunged happily through the drifts.

He ran to her and waded and fell. He laughed and they rolled together and she ate big chunks of snow. She sneezed. He sprawled in the snow and smiled and playfully cuffed her head. His dog licked his face. He clutched the fur at her neck.

Baby Baby Baby.

She woke to a hammering at the door. The latch rattled like a broken toy. His dog sat there, her ears alert and her head cocked, like the dog peering at the Victrola.

A deep voice said, I'll huff and I'll puff and I'll blow your house down.

His dog whined, then yelped, and walked from side to side.

The door burst open and he stood there in his mackinaw and rubber mask.

Scare ya?

She greeted him and happily pushed her paws into his stomach. Her tongue dangled from her grin.

Look what I got.

He brought a transistor radio from behind his back and clicked it on. Then he picked up her paws and waltzed her to the music while she nipped at his fingers. He let her down and she rolled to her back, barking once. He knelt beside her and took off the mask. He touched sweat from his lip.

That was my last job, he said. I'm retired now. This time it's for real.

She stood over him on all fours in bed. His hands were behind his head. He gazed at the rafters as he talked.

I don't know. I guess women are all right, but they're demanding. They always want to make you something you're not. They're critical of how you act. I don't need that.

She nudged his chin and he smiled.

I need you.

He dusted the windowsills and the mantelpiece. He shoveled the fireplace ashes onto a spread of newspapers. Dog hairs collected everywhere and blew away from his broom. He shook his head with annoyance. He washed the dishes and straightened up his room, and he came out carrying a large, gilt-framed mirror.

He set the mirror against the wall and turned the chair around to face it. His dog walked to him, her nails clicking on the floor. She sat at his feet.

He pointed to the mirror. See what I found?

In the mirror he was sitting in the chair in khaki pants and green rubber boots, his legs crossed at the ankles. He was wearing a Pendleton shirt and his hands rested heavily in his lap. Light slanted in from the window.

I wish I had a camera.

He glanced down and squeezed the flesh of his belly. I'm getting fat.

He could see in the mirror that his dog's head was tilted up at him. She dropped her chin on his knee.

Look at us, he said.

* * *

His food tasted bad and he was out of cigarettes. He sat in a stuffed chair all day and watched his dog. Her teeth nitched at her paw. She groomed her tail. She splattered water when she drank from her pan. When he called, she didn't come.

He dealt solitaire and listened to the radio. Once he got up and squashed an insect that was loggily crawling the floor. His dog got up and sniffed it.

He put on his coat, loaded the magazine of his gun, and locked the cabin door from the outside. He waded through snow to the center of the clearing. He saw his dog barking at the cabin window, her paws on the sill, her breath fogging the glass. He carefully lowered the gun on each of the nearer trees. Bark exploded off with each shot. His dog dropped from the window.

He shoved the gun back into the pocket of his coat and filled his lungs with cold air and smiled agreeably. He stamped his boots on the porch step and saw that the door had somehow been unlocked. He went inside and saw his dog sitting primly by the chair. He slammed the door but it didn't close.

She scratched at her neck with a hind leg. It turned the leather collar, jangling the tags.

He grumpily paced the cabin.

Ching ching ching, he said. He bent to her level and said it louder. Ching ching ching ching ching!

His dog regarded him angrily.

She would chew a swatch of hair, then lick it, then chew again.

The coffee in his tin cup was cold. He pushed it across the table, turned on the radio, and watched her teeth burrow higher. He watched for quite a while, then banged his cup. Why are you always eating at yourself?

She looked at him and returned to her thigh.

He went to the kitchen, rinsed his cup, and poured himself more coffee.

You never used to do that.

He saw new flakes of snow tap against the window.

I *hate* that sound.

He kept waking in the middle of the night to see her there beside him on the comforter. She would be silent, observing him, stars of light in her eyes. He would resist touching her and shift to his side.

His dog was off somewhere. He stumbled through the forest, blowing on his fingers. His gun was cold under his belt. He heard his dog growl and wrestle with something. He ran ploddingly through snow, his breath surging, the gun outstretched in both hands. He reached a clearing and saw his dog near a fallen deer, sniffing the red stains in the snow.

Quit that! he shouted. He rocked from side to side, stamping his boots. Quit that quit that quit that!

She stared at him, then trotted ahead, blithely sniffing at snow-laden ferns. She snapped at yellow weeds and dug through snow to the ground.

He ran a few steps and kicked her, knocking her into a tree. She yelped and shied from him and limped ahead, looking over her shoulder with suspicion.

He was awake all night. In the outer room she was growling.

Shut up, for God's sake.

She growled the way she did sometimes when he came too near her food. He threw the covers aside and stood next to the bedroom door. Shut up!

He opened the door and she raised her pitch. She glared at him.

Quiet!

Her nose wrinkled and her teeth showed.

He closed the door and leaned against it.

At dawn she still made the noise, but it was hoarse and dry, like bricks rubbed together. He dressed and went out to her. Her head was on her paws. She growled and lifted her eyebrows and glared at him.

What's the matter, girl? he said soothingly.

Then he reached for her and she grabbed his hand in her jaws. She jerked and shook his arm painfully. He slapped at her but she held. He kicked at her and fell. He yanked a drawer and the lamp table tipped. His gun clattered onto the floor.

She let him go.

The skin was badly torn. He pressed it with his handkerchief. I guess that does it, doesn't it? You and me are finished.

He let his hand bleed under the cold water of the kitchen tap. He couldn't move his fingers. He came out of the kitchen with the bite wrapped.

I mean, do you think I could live with that? Huh?

She looked at him mistrustingly.

He threw his things in the back of the jeep, brushed off snow, and started it. His dog leapt at the jeep windows, scratching the paint, then barked at the caking tires. He put the gun on the seat beside him, and the rubber mask over it. In his rearview mirror he could see her chasing him.

He could brake and throw the jeep into reverse. There'd be a bump and a screech from her. She'd lie in his tracks, shaking with agony. He could then back up over her. The jeep would raise and lower.

He did not do that. But he drove away thinking nothing was too awful for her. She deserved the worst.

He swerved his jeep to the front of a small grocery store. He shut off the engine. He rested his forehead on the steering wheel for a minute, then put on his rubber mask.

His dog slept on the bed in the cabin.

The Sun So Hot I Froze to Death

Everyone is busy here. My wife, Susannah, is wearing a string bikini and a straw hat as she cultivates her victory garden, polishes the watermelon, claws at anthills with a pitchfork. The kid is at his swimming lessons inhaling chlorine and water again. Our housegirl, Mutt, is being joyfully molested in her basement room. And I have a science-fiction story rolled into my typewriter and pages next to it that are just okay. We're big on summer projects.

Along the sill of my window are the ragged tops of green trees and the gray Long Island Sound. All above that is blue. On my desk is an expensive briefcase I haven't shut, emphatic letters I haven't opened, masterpieces I'll never read. The first line of my short story is: "There was once a good guy who was held prisoner by stupid beings on another planet for three years."

It seems like longer. My hero is despondent. He's skin-your-nose sad. At one point a top-dog Tripid suggests he stop brooding, forget whatever's making him so gosh-darn miserable—they talk like that on Planet Dumb—and compile a list of all the reasons he has to be happy despite everything. It's a tremendous success. It turns out my hero is pleased about a lot of things. There's plenty of parking spaces for his car, somehow his socks are always clean, the Tripids serve him buttered popcorn that never seems to creep down between the sofa cushions.

The list really cheers him up.

So: I find my wife desirable. The kid wants to be an astronaut. Mutt gives me a wink now and then. Besides this glorious summer house, I have a six-room apartment in the city that's right on a subway stop. I play squash at noon and haven't chipped a tooth yet. I have only a little trouble sleeping. I am not a writer by profession. Susannah always manages to bring out the best in my performance. I can mix a great martini without a jigger, haggle with garage mechanics, dig burnt muffins out of a toaster without unplugging it. And there are no euphemisms in this house, no toodles or potties or number twos —it's "Dad, my penis is caught in the zipper!" that the kid screams down the hall.

But.

The plumbing is bad here. When most people flush their toilet, it makes a ferocious sound like *Wush!* Ours goes *wickle wickle.* In my own house I'm ashamed to go to the bathroom. Also, the drain in the tub doesn't suck anymore. Hair and scum and a squashed water beetle float around in a pool when the shower's on. To wash your feet you have to close your eyes. And the double sink in the kitchen. Whenever Mutt lets out the dishwater, a soup of vegetables and eggshells churns up on the other side. "Dad," the kid yells. "The sink's throwing up again."

Mutt diets and tans, drinks tea and reeks with lotions. She wastes away on her lounge chair with aluminum foil angling sunlight at her as she poises a glaring reflector underneath her chin. Her bones are like Tinkertoys. My wife wails, "Please please eat something, dear. We're responsible for your well-being."

"Food's such a bore," she says. "I mean, it's just so *redundant.*" When it rains, she makes out with the boy from the lawn service. Even when she's gone, her room groans with pleasure.

Meanwhile the kid is terrified of everything. Phone calls

upset him, he runs howling from the room when I turn on the nightly news, the Sunday comics give him bad dreams. "Kid, kid," I say painfully. "How can you expect to go to prep school if you're constantly terrified? How can you ever expect to be a daddy?" Sometimes I hear the screech as his bed is shoved against the door.

As I already said, I find Susannah desirable. I like watching her bend over. I'm aroused when she files her nails. When she sneezes, she makes a delicate little *choo.* Her lipstick sometimes wavers off her mouth, but even that I find appealing. She likes to zip up my pants. She is, however, continually racked with tears. I have been called to gasoline stations and supermarkets to find her slumped and sobbing on the floor. In her sleep she murmurs, "Caveat emptor."

In "The Prisoner of Planet Dumb," my hero is captured by tiny people, Tripids, with huge brown heads, big mustaches, ears, noses, glasses, funny little hats. They look like Mr. Potato Head. The kid's got one growing roots. They tumble out of the spacecraft, trip on toys carelessly left in the yard, run smack into a fire hydrant; one takes a shot at a glowering swing set while three others shout out warnings to the banged-up garbage cans. The rest apprehend my poor hero and carry him into the saucer "like the coach after a winning season."

Once on the planet, my hero is put in an enormous office, completely alone. Wooden secretaries sit at the desks with big balloons under their sweaters and postage stamps glued to their tongues. Typewriters clatter, telephones ring, a watercooler hums. Daily he's given someone else's cheese Danish with his coffee. Each day at ten the same company newsletter circulates, warning of manpower cuts and the need for expense-account receipts. Each day at four there's an office party with streamers and horns. Giggling and kissing noises are piped in; the elevator is stopped between floors; a wife phones for her husband and a big voice yells, "He just left!"

My hero is fed three times a day but the meals aren't nutritionally balanced. One of the Tripid researchers discovered that the average American male consumes sixty apples per year, eight cloves, seventy-two pounds of flour, thirty-nine ounces of pepper, et cetera. So on his first day there he's issued ninety pounds of sugar to eat and a tin each of nutmeg and paprika. The second day he's given twenty-three pepperoni pizzas and a market basket of oysters. The third day, four hundred and twelve grade-A medium eggs. And so on. They infect him with athlete's foot and earaches. They give him colds that just seem to keep hanging on. They find out his body temperature is ninety-eight point six, so the office is kept at ninety-eight point six. He drinks holy water from Lourdes and wine made from spinach leaves. He's got memory implants of Paris in the spring, a Yankee game that was rained out, someone else's senior prom in Spokane, Washington. They think my hero is perfectly happy.

This story's about sloppy research.

My poor hero is very unhappy. They sense that because he fails to initial their memos and is letting his subscriptions lapse. They dispatch their best physicians, who spray him with an oil that prevents foods from sticking to the skillet. They put corn plasters on his toes and prop up his jaw with a neck brace. They slip him feminine napkins, antacids and pertussives, pills for lower back pain. He remains disconsolate. Several of them try to talk to him, make him open up, but they all sound like potatoes, and my hero can't understand them. Finally he's examined by a physician who learned the English language in a Milwaukee bar. He slaps my hero on the back and shouts, "Whatchu say, you goof? Da wife letcha outa da houze?"

The doctor climbs a stepladder to peer into my hero's ears and eyes. "I'm tellin you palookas," he says, "dis is one big guy we got here. Lookit dem arms. Lookit dem coconuts on him, wouldja?"

The doctor finds nothing wrong. He merely looks at his subject earnestly and asks, "What is dis? You pullin da wool over my eyes or what?"

It's at this juncture that my creative juices peter out.

I'm outside now, in a collapsible lawn chair. I'm wearing swimming trunks that used to fit and a painful jockstrap that's begun to unravel at the waistband. The sun is hot and the pink sweater on my glass of gin is beginning to get soggy. My wife is scolding weeds again. Mutt is recumbent on the diving board with her halter off and her two cute little cupcakes showing. And I'm reading an advertisement for a book about Vincent van Gogh that's just come in the mail. The advertisement flaps in the breeze.

There's a lot about madness and despair in the copy. There are reproductions of van Gogh's paintings. One landscape shows windblown grass and twisted cypress trees, a dark, roiling sky, a lonely path meandering off the canvas. An expert notes the anxiety that caused this painting. Another is a picture of a room. Someone indicates that everything—chairs, pillows, pictures on the wall—is paired, illustrating the solitary artist's acute need for companionship at the time of composition. "You will see," the publishers claim, "how this tortured soul was able to create great art from squalor."

And that brings me to this. I was an M.B.A. student in finance when I married Susannah. We rented an economy apartment and cuddled up by my hi-fi set, and if we scrimped, we could afford a movie once a week and split bargain beers with pictures of mooses and elk on the labels. Life was good, if unglamorous, and we were, as I remember it, very happy. Then I graduated and took a junior executive position in a large bank, and within a year I had three varieties of twelve-year-old Scotch in my kitchen cabinet. Susannah became pregnant, and greed instructed me to resign from the bank for a comptroller slot with a hot company that took just four months to fold. We descended into a neighborhood where the kids carried swords, Susannah did other people's ironing, I drank ale that tasted like fizzed-up tea and had a picture of a platypus on the label. But inside of two years I made a great comeback. Soon I had a metallic-gray foreign car and half a brownstone in the city, and I stocked a wine cellar with bottles that I gingerly rolled and marked every month. We were very, very happy.

It goes up and down like this.

Culprits who'd apparently missed out on the advantages that our great system has to offer stole everything in the brownstone but some leftover platypus ale. The bistro that I owned a piece of was closed by the fussy health department because of spiders in the casserole. I failed to completely survive an income-tax audit. We were hard hit that year, but that was okay, we were young, we were vigorous, we could deal with a setback or two. I paid off my debts and losses, cut down on the Scotch, and limited ourselves to one night of amusement per week, usually topless dancers and tacos. Soon we were rolling again. I got into a high-tech company at ground level and scored big on a merger. I was tapped to join a partnership investing in treasury bills—one of those can't-lose propositions. Then one day I said, "Look, Susannah, we have all this dough stashed away and what's it earning, eight and a half percent? Why don't we make it really work for us?" Which, of course, is the same as saying, "Jeepers, everything's going so swell, why don't we screw it up?"

So we overextended our credit and bought this summer

house and this shrinking housegirl, Mutt, and riding lessons for the kid, which he hates, and swimming lessons so he can swallow the pool. And the plumbing's bad here and the mosquitoes whine at your ears at night and we all have pathetic summer projects: victory gardens, chocolate suntans, science-fiction stories. Yesterday I came out here with a book, planning to sit down for a good read, but the world was so much with me that I spent all of the afternoon just staring at the hedge.

The yard gate swings. The kid drags through, rubbing his eyes, his wet swimming trunks for some reason cocked rakishly on his head. Susannah walks to him; he sprints and buries his face in her bikini. "Who did this to you?" she demands, and he blurts some preschool language. Mutt and her boyfriend are in the pool going at it. I take van Gogh with me to the house. The last thing I hear Susannah say is, "Did you *tell* the lifeguard you were drowning? Well, honey, how do you expect him to know these things if you never speak up? You've got to put your best foot forward!"

Upstairs I typed this about my hero: "He fixed his eyes on the Tripids' large pink noses and black glasses as they murmured to each other in gobbledygook. After a silence he swelled his chest and made a heartfelt speech, telling his audience how terribly mixed-up Planet Dumb was."

Just that much wore me out.

At dinner the kid decided to eat his food without utensils or fingers. He poured his milk in a bowl and lapped at it. His head burrowed into his coleslaw. He pushed his corn around with his nose. I would have preferred it otherwise. Mutt was facing me, her lips as pinched as a dime, decomposing. I imagined those hungry cells of hers jumping ship by the thousands. Since she wasn't eating, she could talk without mispronouncing a word. She said, "I used to work at this nursing home, you know? And there was this snowy-haired old lady who just sort of *disintegrated* one year. I'd walk past her room in the morning and hear her shout, 'Welp, that's it for the kidneys!' On another day she might squawk to herself, 'So it's the feet now, is it? Good riddance!' It seemed every week she'd lose the use of something else and *herald* it to herself: spleen, eyelid, pancreas, hip. The doctors could never find anything wrong, but still she declined. I visited her in the hospital and she looked dreadful. She'd kick the bucket that very night. Like a dope I asked, 'How are you feeling now, Meg?' And in this tired, creaky voice she said, 'Oh. Pretty. Good.' "

The kid snarfled at his hot dogs.

Susannah said, "When I was a little girl, there was a farmer down the way with a henhouse and he'd let his chickens out to peck at the gravel on the road. Oh, golly, there must've been two dozen chickens to start with, but one by one they got creamed by automobiles. I kept appealing to the farmer, 'Shouldn't you be more cautious with your birds?' I'd say, 'Couldn't you tend them somewhere else?' He'd merely chuckle and answer, 'Those chickens aren't as stupid as they look. Those chickens do fine out there.' The last time I saw him he was still grinning from his front-porch rocker, overseeing his last skittish hen."

The kid wiped his face with the tablecloth. "Are the elves Santa's children?"

I trudged up the stairs to the dark study with my typewriter in it. I hit the switch on the desk lamp and shook it until the light bulb flickered on. I changed the ribbon in the machine.

My hero tells the people of Planet Dumb that they've made a ridiculous mistake. They were probably looking for a new frontier, he says. They were probably searching for a specimen, an example, a typical human being, and inadvertently picked up the one man on Earth who was sui generis, unique. He tells them, everyone else is helpless. Most people on Earth wake up in the morning wondering what they can do to make themselves miserable. From the moment they're born, they play games where nine people try to sit on eight chairs. Hundreds of people buy chances for one puny prize. They punish themselves in amusement parks. They don't have gills but they try to swim. They have sports in which a person is supposed to carry a ball from one place to another, but instead of being careful about it, the player tosses it in the air, bounces it, negligently hands it to other people. And Earthlings are constantly at war with their bodies. Those who haven't given up eating are increasing themselves with gluttony. Or they're developing stammers and tics and sweaty palms. They're afraid of airplanes and snakes and growing old, of dogs and earthquakes and fires and guns, and of being unable to make a commitment. If there aren't any bathrooms around, that's when they have to go. Only when they've taken a forkful of food do they sneeze. They have Sunday pipes and trick knees and allergies; they have cricks in their necks and butterflies in their stomachs and crazy bones near their elbows.

My hero pauses, waiting for his interpreter to catch up. The potato heads of Planet Dumb are crying their many eyes out. Very sadly my hero says, "I don't suggest you go there."

The Tripid physician complains, "But we been spendin' a lotta moola on da expeditions, ya know? We don't wanna waste all dat green stuff."

My hero nods grimly. He knows how dat is. He looks out the picture window with its Halloween and Valentine and Christmas decorations. Below there's the buzzing of the bees and the cigarette trees, the sugarcoated fountains.

I have no idea what he'll say next.

I sat there and smoked a South American cigar down to the

stub and no words came. I walked to the bedroom. Susannah was in the bathroom running water and splashing on foo-foo. On the bed was a newsmagazine, its pages wrinkled with tears. I noticed for the first time that there were two chairs in the room, two reading lamps and vanities, that the pictures were paired on the wall. I shut off the light and let the dark diffuse itself for a while, then wandered into the victory garden, slapped mosquitoes, and sipped brandy in the kitchen as I filled up one side of the double sink, let it empty, and watched the peach skins and coffee grounds gurgle up on the other side.

I turned off the faucet and waited for the sink's garbage to settle, then crept down to Mutt's room. The light was on. I rapped on the door. "Mutt," I said. "It's me."

I could hear the swish of her slippers. She asked in her emaciated voice, "What do you want?"

"I want to discuss something." I listened to her silence. "I won't feel you up, Mutt. I promise. It's about my summer project."

She opened the door and looked at me as if she were about to expire. I sagged against the door frame, done in by her skeleton. "I've got this story," I said, and explained everything about it. I was stuck, I said. I had problems.

Mutt said, "Well, it's not a story really, is it? I mean, it doesn't have a plot. It's just comments, you know?"

"Yeah, that's what I'm stuck on."

She thought a moment. She was wearing a sweatshirt with a portrait of Emily Dickinson on it. She said, "Maybe you ought to have this guy decide not to hassle it any longer. Maybe you could make him content with his portion in life."

I must have sagged a little farther down the door frame.

"I mean, maybe what you should say is that other worlds are pretty much identical when you get down to the nitty-gritty.

Like, if one's screwed up, it could be they all are. That's what science fiction's all about, isn't it?"

I was rather mute for a minute.

She threw some bleached hair off her forehead. "Maybe you should ask the kid. Intergalactic stuff makes me cross-eyed."

"Yeah," I said. "Maybe I'll do that."

I tramped up the stairs to the kid's room, opened the door, and stood over his breathing, brushing his bangs away. They're trying to teach him to float. The girl instructor stands beside him in the pool, he flops forward and sinks like a stone. "Bravo!" she yells. "Just like a jellyfish!" The kid bursts to the surface wiping his eyes and coughing.

"Kid," I whispered. "Kid."

"Mister Sand Man?" he asked.

I switched on the clown light.

"Oh."

I sat with him slumped and drowsing under my arm.

I told him I was writing a story about an astronaut trapped on a planet in outer space. (I shook the kid awake.) The astronaut didn't like the planet he came from very much (I pinched the kid) but doubted he'd like anyplace else much better. I told him it seemed to me I had a lot of options for my hero but couldn't decide on which.

The kid groggily told me he'd seen a movie like that. The guy eventually leads an attack on his former planet but gets zapped by a laser beam aimed by a girlfriend he'd jilted. There was also a TV show once in which the guy went through all those troubles only to find out that it was just another in a series of preflight tests; the scientists wanted to study his reactions to various stimuli. The kid said a similar story had the Earthling become king of a planet where he ruled magnificently for eons, then foreign robots attacked and by mistake took the top man as a specimen of the culture. The hook is, when he's on board the transport, he asks where he's going and one of the robots answers, "Earth." In still another, the guy finds out this is his punishment for a crime he thought he'd gotten away with. The kid went on describing other versions. It was apparently a common theme.

"Thanks, kid," I said. "You've been a lot of help."

I tucked him in.

"Dad?"

"Yes, kid?"

"I think you should make it happy."

I patted him on the head.

I went to the room where my wife was biting her pillow. I brushed my teeth, unbuttoned my natty shirt, and washed in cold water, whistling something catchy. My watch glowed in the dark. It was midnight. If she asked what time it was, I'd say, "Tomorrow." That always sounds terrific. Tomorrow I'll make my hero content with his portion in life. I'll give him two chairs, two pillows, a double bed, two van Goghs on the wall. Then maybe I'll give him somebody to love. Maybe I'll give him Mutt. Tomorrow I'll make it happy.

Susannah, don't you cry.

Can I Just Sit Here for a While?

He was called a traveler, and that was another thing he loved about the job. If you wanted the hairy truth, Rick Bozack couldn't put his finger on any one thing that made his job such a clincher. It might have been his expense account or the showroom smell of his leased Oldsmobile or the motel rooms—God, the motel rooms: twin double beds, a stainless-steel Kleenex dispenser, and a bolted-down color TV topped with cellophane-wrapped peppermints that the maid left after she cleaned. He loved the coffee thermos the waitress banged down on his table at breakfast, he loved the sweat on his ice-water glass, he loved the spill stains blotting through the turned-over check, and he loved leaving tips of twenty percent even when the girl was slow and sullen and splashed coffee on his newspaper. His sales, his work, his vocation, that was all bonus. The waiting, the handshakes, the lunches, The Close, jeepers, that was just icing.

If you asked Rick Bozack what he did for a living, he wouldn't come out with a song and dance about selling expensive incubators and heart and kidney machines for Doctor's Service Supply Company, Indianapolis. Not off the top of his head he wouldn't. Instead he'd flash on a motel lobby with all the salesmen in their sharp, tailored suits, chewing sugarless gum, while the sweet thing behind the counter rammed a roller over a plastic credit card and after-shaves mixed in the air. It was goofy when he thought about it, but walking out through those fingerprinted glass doors, throwing his briefcase onto the red bucket seat, scraping the ice off the windshield, and seeing all those other guys out there in the parking lot with him, scowling, chipping away at their wipers, blowing on their fingers, sliding their heater control to defrost, Rick felt like a team player again, like he was part of a fighter squadron.

What was this *Death of a Salesman* crap? he'd say. What were they feeding everybody about the hard life on the road? You'd have to be zonkers not to love it.

Then Rick had a real turnaround. A college buddy said something that really clobbered him. Rick and his wife, Jane, had returned to South Bend, his home, for the Notre Dame alumni picnic, where they collided with people they hadn't even thought of in years. They sat all night at a green picnic table with baked beans and hot dogs and beer, laughing so much that their sides hurt, having a whale of a time. They swapped pictures of their kids, and Rick drew a diagram of an invention he might go ahead and get patented, a device that would rinse out messy diapers for daddies right there in the toilet bowl. He told all comers that he was thirty-four years old and happily married, the father of two girls, and he woke up every morning with a sapsucker grin on his face. Then Mickey Hogan, this terrific buddy in advertising who had just started up his own firm, said you don't know the thrill of business until it's your own, until every sale you make goes directly into your pocket and not to some slob back in the home office.

This guy Hogan wasn't speaking *de profundis* or anything, but Rick was really blown away by what he said. It was one of those fuzzy notions you carry with you for years, and then it's suddenly there, it's got shape and bulk and annoying little edges that give you a twinge whenever you sit down. That's how it was.

He and Jane talked about it all the way back to their three-bedroom apartment on Rue Monet in Indianapolis. "How much of what I earn actually makes my wallet any fatter? What do I have besides a measly income? When am I going to get off my duff and get something going on my own?"

Jane was great about it. She said she loved him and she'd go along with whatever his choice was, but she had watched him waste himself at Doctor's Service Supply Company. She knew he was a great salesman, but he had all the earmarks of being a fantastic manager too. She had been hoping he'd come up with something like this but didn't want to influence Rick one way or the other. "I don't want to push" were her words.

Jane's enthusiasm put a fire under Rick, and he began checking things out on the sly: inventory costs, car leases and office-space rentals, government withholding tax and social-security regulations, and though it seemed dopey and juvenile, the couple decided that they'd both stop smoking, watch their caloric intake, avoid between-meal treats, and exercise regularly. Sure, they were mainly concerned with hashing out this new business venture, but how far afield was it to take stock of yourself, your physical condition, to discipline yourself and set goals? That was Rick's thinking, and Jane thought he was "right on the money."

The two of them let a half gallon of ice cream melt down in the sink, got out the scale and measuring tape, bought matching running outfits, and they took turns with Tracy and Connor at breakfast while one of them jogged around the block.

And Rick was no slouch when he was out on the road. He jogged in cold cities and on gravel county roads and in parking lots of Holiday Inns. Other salesmen would run toward him in wristbands and heavy sweatshirts, and Rick would say, "How's it going?"

"How's it going?" they'd reply.

Rick imagined millions of joggers saying the same thing to each other. It felt as good as the days of the Latin Mass, when you knew it was just as incomprehensible in Dusseldorf, West Germany, as it was in Ichikawa, Japan.

On one of his business trips to South Bend, Rick jogged on the cinder track of Notre Dame's great football stadium, where who should he see but Walter Herdzina, a terrific buddy of his! Rick was flabbergasted. The guy had aged—who hadn't?—but he remembered Rick like it was only yesterday, even recited some wild dorm incidents that Rick had put the eraser to. The two men ran an eight-minute mile together and leaned on their knees and wiped their faces on their sweatshirts, and after they had discussed pulse rates, refined sugar, and junk foods, Walter said, "You ought to move back to South Bend."

Jane, bless her heart, kept bringing up South Bend too. It was smack in the middle of his territory and a natural home base, but he had never really thought about South Bend much before the alumni picnic. When the company hired Rick, they had assumed he'd want to settle in a giant metropolis like Indianapolis so he could have some jam-packed leisure time, and he had never mentioned his roots farther north. And it wasn't unusual for Rick to spend two or three days in South Bend and not give anyone except his mom a call. But now there seemed to be a come-as-you-are feeling, a real hometown warmth he hadn't noticed before.

In September he closed a deal with a gynecological clinic that would earn him six thousand dollars, what salesmen called the Cookies. But instead of immediately driving home for a wingding celebration, Rick decided to make some business phone contacts—thank yous, actually—and ride out his hot streak, see what fell in his lap. He stopped in the lobby of a downtown bank building to use its plush telephone booths, then, on an impulse, he asked to see someone in the business-loan department. A receptionist said a loan vice president could see him and Rick walked into his office and—how's this for a coincidence?—the vice president was Walter Herdzina! You could've knocked Rick over with a feather. "Boy," he said, "you're really going places."

Walter smirked. "They'll probably wise up and have me sweeping the floors before my pen's out of ink."

Rick spoke off the top of his head. He had been with Doctor's Service Supply Company, Indianapolis, for six years, after three years with Johnson & Johnson. He'd built up a pretty good reputation in Indiana and southern Michigan, and now and then got offers from industries in Minnesota and California to switch over to a district manager's job and a cozy boost in salary. What he wanted to know was, could a banker like Walter, with years of experience and a shrewd eye for markets and money potential, give him a good solid reason why he shouldn't go into business for himself? Crank up his own distributorship?

Walter Herdzina glanced at his watch and suggested they go out for lunch.

Rick figured that meant *You gotta be kidding.* "This is pretty off-the-wall," he said. "I really haven't had time to analyze the pros and cons or work up any kind of prospectus."

Walter put a heavy hand on his shoulder. "How about us talking about it at lunch?"

Mostly they talked about rugby. It had been a maiden sport at Notre Dame when they played it, but now it was taking the college by storm. Why? Because when you got right down to it, men liked seeing what they were made of, what sort of guts they had.

"Lessons like that stick," Walter said. "I get guys coming

to me with all kinds of schemes, packages, brilliant ideas. And I can tell right away if they were ever athletes. If they never really hurt themselves to win at something, well, I'm a little skeptical."

Walter ordered the protein-rich halibut; Rick had the dieter's salad.

Rick told the banker traveler stories. He told him anecdotes about salesmanship. He had sold insurance and mutual funds in the past and, for one summer, automobiles, and he had discovered a gimmick—well, not that, a *tool*—that hadn't failed him yet. It was called the Benjamin Franklin Close.

"Say you get a couple who're wavering over the purchase of a car. You take them into your office and close the door and say, 'Do you know what Benjamin Franklin would do in a case like this?' That's a toughie for them so you let them off the hook. You take out a tablet and draw a line down the center of the page, top to bottom. 'Benjamin Franklin,' you say, 'would list all the points in favor of buying this car, and then he'd list whatever he could against it. Then he'd total everything up.' You're the salesman, you handle the benefits. You begin by saying, 'So okay, you've said your old car needs an overhaul. That's point one. You've said you want a station wagon for the kids; that's point two. You've told me that particular shade of brown is your favorite.' And so on. Once you've written down your pitches, you flip the tablet around and hand across the pen. 'Okay,' you tell them. 'Now Benjamin Franklin would write down whatever he had *against* buying that car.' And you're silent. As noiseless as you can be. You don't say boo to them. They stare at that blank side of the paper and they get flustered. They weren't expecting this at all. Maybe the wife will say, 'We can't afford the payments,' and the husband will hurry up and scribble that down. Maybe he'll say, 'It's really more car than we need for city driving.' He'll glance at you for approval, but you won't even nod your head. You've suddenly turned to stone. Now they're really struggling. They see two reasons against and twelve reasons for. You decide to help them out. You say, 'Was it the color you didn't like?' Of course not, you dope. You put that down as point three in favor. But the wife will say, 'Oh, no, I like that shade of brown a lot.' You sit back in your chair and wait. You wait four or five minutes if you have to, until they're really uncomfortable, until you've got them feeling like bozos. Then you take the tablet from them and make a big show of making the tally. They think you're an idiot, anyway; counting out loud won't surprise them. And when you've told them they have twelve points in favor, two points against, you sit back in your chair and let that sink in. You say, 'What do you think Benjamin Franklin would do in this situation?' You've got them cornered and they know it and they can't think of a way out because there's only one way and they rarely consider it. Pressed against the wall like that the only solution is for the man or woman to say, 'I—just—don't—*feel*—like—it—now.' All the salesman can do then is recapitulate. If they want to wait, if the vibes don't feel right, if they don't sense it's the appropriate thing to do, they've got him. 'I just don't feel like it now.' There's no way to sell against that."

Walter grinned. He thought Rick might have something. Even in outline his distributorship had real sex appeal.

So that afternoon Rick drove south to Indianapolis with his CB radio turned down so he wouldn't have all the chatter, and he picked up a sitter for his two little roses and took Jane out for prime rib, claiming he wanted to celebrate the six-thousand-dollar commission. But after they had toasted the Cookies, he sprang the deal on her, explained everything about the lunch and Walter's positive reaction, how it all fit together, fell into place, shot off like a rocket. And what it all boiled down to was, they could move up to South Bend, buy a house, and in two months, three months, a year, maybe he'd have his very own medical instruments and supplies company.

Jane was ecstatic. Jane was a dynamo. While Rick did the dog-and-pony show for his boss and got him to pick up the tab for a move to the heart of Rick's territory, Jane did the real work of selecting their two-story home and supervising the movers. Then Rick walked Tracy and little Connor from house to house down the new block in South Bend, introducing himself and his daughters to their new neighbors. There were five kids the same age on just one side of the street! Rick imagined Tracy and Connor as gorgeous teenagers at a backyard party with hanging lanterns and some of Rick's famous punch, and maybe two thousand four hundred boys trying to get a crack at his girls.

He drank iced tea with a stockbroker who crossed his legs and gazed out the window as Tracy tried to feed earthworms to his spaniel.

"Plenty of playmates," said Rick.

"This place is a population bomb."

"Yeah, but I love kids, don't you? I get home from a week on the road and there's nothing I like better than to roll on the floor a few hours with them."

The man spit ice cubes back into his glass. "But your kids are girls!" the man said.

Rick shrugged. "I figure my wife will tell me when I should stop it."

What'd he think, that Rick would be copping feels, pawing them through their training bras? Maybe South Bend had its creepy side, after all. Maybe a few of these daddies could bear some scrutiny.

Rick gave a full report to his wife, Jane, as they sat down with beers on the newly carpeted floor of the living room, telling her about all the fascinating people he had met in just a casual swing down the block. Jane said, "I don't know how you can just go knocking on doors and introducing yourself. I can't think of a single thing to say when I'm with strangers."

Rick said, "That's one of the things that comes with being a traveler. You just assume you're welcome until someone tells you otherwise."

But how did that square with the uneasiness Rick Bozack felt with his old chum Mickey Hogan? A year ago Mickey had been a high-priced copywriter, but then he had gone out on a limb to take over a smaller house that had been strictly an art and layout jobber, and the gamble had paid off in spades. Mickey turned the firm into a real comer in South Bend, what they call in the trade a "hot shop."

Of course, Mickey had always been a brain. They had been rugby buddies at Notre Dame, and they used to shoot snooker together and swap tennis shoes and generally pal around like they were in a rowdy television commercial for some brand of light beer. Now Mickey was almost skinny and as handsome as Sergio Franchi, and taking full advantage of it, don't let anybody kid you. They had doubled to the Notre Dame/Army game last season, and Mickey brought along a knockout who kept sneaking her hand under Mickey's blue leg warmer. Rick couldn't keep his eyes off her. Even Jane noticed it. "Boy, I bet she put lead in your pencil," she said.

So Rick was delighted but amazed when in February Mickey said he'd make the third for a terrific bunch of seats at the Notre Dame/Marquette basketball game. Mickey was even sitting on the snow-shoveled steps of his condominium, like some company president on the skids, when Rick pulled up along the curb. And now Mickey was smoking a black cigarillo as Rick told him how astonished he was these days to see that everyone he met was about his age; they had all risen to positions of authority, and he was finding they could do him some good. You always thought it was just your father who could throw a name around. Now Rick was doing it himself, and getting results! "I'm really enjoying my thirties," Rick said, and then smiled. "I've got twenty credit cards in my wallet, and I don't get acne anymore."

Mickey just looked at him, bored.

"Okay, maybe not twenty credit cards, but my complexion's all cleared up."

Mickey sighed and looked out the window.

Rick had forgotten how much of a jerk Mickey could be.

Rick kept the engine running and shoved the Captain and Tenille in his tape deck so Mickey could nestle in with some good tunes, then he pressed the door chimes to a house the Herdzinas had just bought: eighty thousand smackers, minimum. A small girl in pink underpants opened the door.

"Hi," said Rick in his Nice Man voice.

The girl shoved a finger up her nose.

Karen Herdzina hugged him hello. The hugging was a phenomenon that was totally new to South Bend and Rick never felt he handled it well. He lingered a bit too long with women, and with men he was on the lookout for a quick takedown and two points on the scoreboard.

"I'll put some hustle into Walt," she said. "Tell him to get it in gear."

Walter came out of the bedroom with a new shirt he was ripping the plastic off of. "Mickey in the car?"

Rick nodded. "But it really belts out the heat."

Walter unpinned the sleeves and the cardboards and shoved the trash into a paper sack that had the cellophane wrappers of record albums in it.

"Look at that," he said. "My wife. She goes out spending my hard-earned money on records. The Carpenters. John Denver. I don't know what gets into her sometimes."

"I kind of enjoy John Denver," said Rick.

"See?" Karen called.

As they walked to the thrumming Oldsmobile, Walter leaned into Rick, fanning three tickets out like a heart-stopping poker hand. "How about these beauties, Richard?"

"Wow! What do I owe ya?"

He frowned and pushed the tickets back into his wallet. "*De nada,*" said Walter. "Buy me a beer."

As Rick drove, he and Walter talked about their budding families. You could see it was driving Mickey bananas. Here he was a bachelor, giving up a night when he could've probably had some make-out artist in the sack, and all he was hearing was talk about drooling and potties and cutting new teeth. So as he climbed up onto the highway Rick introduced the topic of college basketball, and Walter scrunched forward to talk about the Marquette scoring threat, but Mickey interrupted to ask Walter if he knew that Rick was considering his own distributorship.

"Hell," the banker said, "I'm the one who put the gleam in his eye." He settled into the backseat and crossed his kid leather gloves in his lap. "I think that's a tremendous opportunity, Rick. Where've you gone with it lately?"

"He's been testing the waters," said Mickey.

"I've sort've put it on the back burner until Jane and the kids get a better lay of the land," said Rick. "I think it might be a pretty good setup, though. Almost no time on the road and very little selling. I'll see what it's like to stay around the house and carry those canvas money bags up to the teller's window."

Walter grew thoughtful. "I read somewhere that every person who starts a new business makes at least one horrible mistake. Something really staggering. If you get through that and you don't get kayoed, I guess you got it made."

They were quiet then for several minutes, as if in mourning for all those bankrupts who had been walloped in the past. The tape player clicked onto the second side. Mickey tapped one of his black cigarillos on his wrist.

"You really like those things?" Rick asked.

Mickey lit it with the car lighter. "Yep," Mickey said. "I like them a lot."

Rick turned into the Notre Dame parking lot. "Since I gave up smoking, I notice it all the time. This health kick's really made a difference. I'm down two notches on my belt, my clothes don't fit, and I want to screw all the time now." He switched off the ignition. "How's that for a side benefit?"

Mickey said, "You smile a lot, you know that?"

It was just an okay game, nothing spectacular as far as Rick was concerned. In fact, if you conked him on the head, he might even have said it was boring. Where was the teamwork? Where was the give-and-take? A couple of black guys were out there throwing up junk shots, making the white guys look like clowns, propelling themselves up toward the hoop like they were taking stairs three at a time. It went back and forth like that all night, and except for the spine-tingling Note Dame songs, except for the perky cheerleaders and the silver flask of brandy Mickey passed up and down the row, Rick caught himself wishing he was in a motel room somewhere eating cheese slices on crackers.

At the final buzzer the three guys filed out with the crowd, giving the nod to other old buddies and asking them how tricks were. The Oldsmobile engine turned slowly with cold before it caught, and as Rick eyed the oil pressure gauge Mickey removed the Captain and Tenille from the tape deck. Mr. Sophisticated.

Rick took the crosstown and shoved in a tape of Tony Orlando. Walter was paging through one of the catalogs for Doctor's Service Supply Company, Indianapolis, when he noticed a pizza parlor was still open, how did that sound? Rick admitted it didn't blow the top of his head off, but he guessed he could give it a whirl. Mickey just sat there like wax.

Rick swerved in next to a souped-up Ford with big rear wheels and an air scoop on the hood. SECRET STORM was printed in maroon on the fender. As the three walked up to the pizza parlor's entrance, Rick saw them mirrored by the big windows, in blue shirts and rep ties and cashmere topcoats, with scowls in their eyes and gray threads in their hair and gruesome mortgages on their houses, and not one of them yet living up to his full potential.

Walter stood with Rick at the counter as he ordered a twelve-inch combination pizza. An overhead blower gave them pompadours. "Hey," said Rick, "that was fun."

Walter showed three fingers to a girl at the beer taps. He said, "My wife encourages me to go out with you boys. She thinks it'll keep me from chasing tail."

Rick wished he had been somewhere else when Walter said that. It said everything about the guy.

Mickey walked to the cigarette machine and pressed every button, then, deep in his private *Weltschmerz,* he wandered past a sign that read, THIS SECTION CLOSED. Rick backed away from the counter with the beers, sloshing some on his coat, and made his way to the dark and forbidden tables where Mickey was moodily sitting.

Mickey frowned. "How long are we going to dawdle here?"

"You got something you wanted to do?"

"There's *always* something to do, Rick."

A girl in a chef's hat seated an elderly couple in the adjoining area. She had pizza menus that she crushed to her breast as she sidestepped around benches toward the drinking buddies, bumping the sign that read THIS SECTION CLOSED, schoolmarm disapproval in her eyes.

Mickey rocked back in his chair. "Can I just sit here for a while? Would it ruin your day if I just sat here?"

The girl stopped and threw everything she had into the question and then shrugged and walked back to the cash register.

Rick almost smacked his forehead, he was that impressed. Mickey could get away with stuff that would land Rick in jail or small-claims court.

Soon he and Walter tore into a combination pizza, achieving at once a glossy burn on the roofs of their mouths. Mickey must not have wanted any. He seemed to have lost the power of speech. After a while Walter asked if either of them had read a magazine article about a recent psychological study of stress.

Rick asked, "How do you find time to *read?*"

"I can't," Walter said. "Karen gets piles of magazines in the mail, though, and she gives me digests of them at dinner."

Mickey looked elsewhere as Walter explained that this particular study showed that whenever a person shifted the furniture of his life in any significant way at all, he or she was increasing the chances of serious illness. Change for the better? Change for the worse? Doesn't matter. If your spouse dies, you get a hundred points against you. You get fired, that's fifty. You accomplish something outstanding, really excellent, still you get something in the neighborhood of thirty points tacked on to your score. The list went on and on. Mortgages counted, salary bonuses, shifts in eating habits. "You collect more than three hundred of these puppies in a year," Walter said, "and it's time to consult a shrink."

Neither Walter nor Rick could finish the pizza, so Rick asked the kitchen help for a sack to take the remains home in. Then the three men walked out into the night, gripping their collars at their necks, their ears crimped by the cold. It was getting close to zero. Rick could hear it in the snow.

There were three boys in Secret Storm, each dangling pizza over his mouth and getting cheese on his chin.

Rick opened the car door on his side and bumped the trim on the souped-up Ford. He smiled and shrugged his shoulders at the kid on the passenger's side.

The kid called him a son of a bitch.

Mickey immediately walked around the car. "What'd he call you?"

"Nothing, Mickey. He was kidding."

But Mickey was already thumping the kid's car door with his knee. "I want to hear what you called him!"

The door bolted open against Mickey's cashmere coat, soiling it, and a kid bent out, unsnapping a Catholic high school letterman's jacket. Before he had the last snap undone, Mickey punched him in the neck. The kid grabbed his throat and coughed. Mickey held his fists like cocktail glasses.

Walter stood in the cold with his gloved hands over his ears as Rick tried to pull Mickey away from the fracas. The kid hooked a fist into Rick's ear and knocked him against the car. Mickey tackled the kid and smacked him against the pavement. Dry snow fluffed up and blew. Rick covered his sore ear and Mickey tried to pin the kid's arms with his knees, but the other boys were out of the Ford by then and urging their friend to give Mickey a shellacking. And at once it was obvious to Rick that the boys weren't aware they were dealing with three strapping men in the prime of their lives, men who had played rugby at Notre Dame when it was just a maiden sport.

Rick and Walter managed to untangle Mickey and grapple him inside the car. Rick spun his wheels on the ice as he gunned the Oldsmobile out of the parking lot. One of the kids kicked his bumper, and another pitched a snowball that *whumped* into the trunk.

Rick said, "I don't believe you, Mickey."

Mickey was just getting his wind back. "You don't believe what?" Mickey said.

"You're thirty-five years old, Mick! You don't go banging high-school kids around."

Walter wiped the rear window with his glove. "Oh, no," he groaned.

Mickey turned around. "Are they following us?"

"Maybe their home's in the same direction," said Rick.

Mickey jerked open the door. Cold air flapped through the catalogs of Doctor's Service Supply Company, Indianapolis. "Let me out," Mickey said.

"Are you kidding?" Rick gave him a look that spoke of his resolute position on the question while communicating his willingness to compromise on issues of lesser gravity.

And yet Mickey repeated, "Let me out."

"What are you going to do?"

"Shut up and let me out of this car."

Walter said, "I think those are *Catholic* kids, Michael."

Rick made a right-hand turn, and so did the souped-up Ford. They were on a potholed residential street of ivied brick homes and one-car garages.

Mickey pushed the door open and scraped off the top of a snow pile. He leaned out toward the curb like a sick drunk about to lose it until Rick skidded slantwise on the ice pack and stopped. Then Mickey hopped out and slipped on the ice and sprawled against the right front door of the Ford.

The boy who'd called Rick a son of a bitch cracked his

skull on the door frame trying to get out, and he sat back down pretty hard, with pain in his eyes and both hands rubbing his stocking cap.

"All right, you bastard," the driver, a big bruiser, said, and lurched out, tearing off *his* letterman's jacket. The kid in the backseat squeezed out through the passenger door as if they were only stopping for gas. He stripped a stick of gum and folded it into his mouth, then put his hands in his jeans pockets. Rick walked over to him and the kid's eyes slid. "Bob's going to make mincemeat out of your friend, man."

Mickey and the kid named Bob stepped over a yard hedge and Mickey was hanging his coat on a clothesline pole. Walter was on the sidewalk, stamping snow off his wing tips, apparently hoping he couldn't be seen.

Rick sought a pacifying conversational gambit. "How about this weather?" Rick asked the kid. "My nose is like an ice cube."

The kid smiled. "Colder than a witch's tit, ain't it?"

The kid was in Rick's pocket. Rick still had the goods, all right; spells he hadn't tapped yet.

Mickey and the boy named Bob were closing together in the night-blue snow, like boxers about to touch gloves, when Mickey swung his right fist into the kid's stomach and the kid collapsed like a folding chair. "Ow! *Ow!*" he yelled. "Oh, man, where'd you hit me? Jeez, that hurts!"

A light went on in an upstairs bedroom.

The passenger got out of the souped-up car, still holding his stocking cap, and the kid next to Rick tripped through deep snow to help Bob limp back to the Ford. "Get me to a hospital quick!"

One of them said, "Oh, you're okay, Bob."

"You don't know, man! I think the dude might've burst my appendix or something! I think he was wearing a ring!"

Mickey carefully put on his coat and sucked the knuckles

of his right hand when he sat down inside the Oldsmobile. As Rick drove to Mickey's condominium, Mickey pressed a bump on his forehead and put on his gloves again.

"What made you want to do that, Mick?"

Mickey was red-eyed. "Are you going to let some punk call you a son of a bitch?"

Rick slapped the steering wheel. "Of course! I do it all the *time!* Is that supposed to destroy you or something?"

Mickey just looked at the floor mats or out the window. He jumped out when Rick parked in front of his place, the sack of cold pizza clamped under his arm. He didn't say good-bye.

Walter Herdzina moved up to the front seat and brought the seat belt over to its catch. "Whew! What an evening, huh?"

"I feel like I've run twenty miles."

Walter crossed his legs and jiggled his shoe until Rick drove onto Walter's driveway, where he shook Rick's hand and suggested they do this again sometime, and also wished him good luck in getting his business out of the starting gate.

The light was on in the upstairs bedroom of the Bozacks' blue Colonial home. Jane had switched the lights off downstairs. Rick let himself in with the milk-box key and hung up his coat. He opened the refrigerator door and peered in for a long time, and then Rick found himself patting his pockets for cigarettes. He went to the dining-room breakfront and found an old carton of Salems next to the Halloween cocktail napkins.

He got a yellow ruled tablet and a pen from the desk and sat down in the living room with a lit cigarette. He printed VENTURE at the top. He drew a line down the center of the paper and numbered the right-hand side from one to twelve. After a few minutes there, Jane came down the stairs in her robe.

"Rick?"

"What?"

"I wanted to know if it was you."

"Who else would it be?"

"Why don't you come up? I'm only reading magazines."

"I think I'd like to just sit here for a while."

"In the *dark?*"

He didn't speak.

"Are you smoking?"

"Yep. I was feeling especially naughty."

She was silent. She stood with both feet on the same step. "You're being awfully mysterious."

"I just want to sit here for a while. Can I do that? Can I just sit here for a while?"

Jane climbed back up the stairs to their bedroom.

Rick stared at the numbered page. Why quit the team? Why risk the stress? Why give up all those Cookies?

If pressed against the wall, he'd say, "I just don't feel like it now."

The Boogeyman

The Corporal pushes aside the green case of machetes and six crates of assorted shoes and moves to the lightless rear of the pawnshop. Ancient muskets and spotted brown swords are hanging from the ceiling. The Corporal peers at one coat for a long time and then points to it. The pawnshop owner looks up and nods. He says in his own language that the coat is not only a bargain but exactly what a good soldier needs.

"How much is it?"

The man creeps through the junk underfoot and removes the red coat from its hanger. It appears to be only a helicopter pilot's jacket made of resplendent red silk, but the man says, "Yes, plenty important coat." The pawnshop owner flips the coat over. Embroidered across the top is the phrase "Live Free or Die," and below that is a green dragon with wings sewn in rainbow colors. Curling out of its mouth are yellow flames.

"Yeah," the Corporal says. "That's what I want. How much is it?"

The little man squints his eyes at the Corporal. "I *give* it to you, soldier."

The Corporal drinks a green beer and swivels on a high bar stool to tell a girl in net stockings stories about how he split a private's lip clean past his nose with only one punch, how he rolled grenades into a sergeant's tent, how he shot a machine gun overhead and then walked inside the anarchy of slugs pelting down like rain.

She listens, openmouthed, and then sips from his glass. "You not so tough," she says. "I hear plenty worse than that."

The Corporal says, "I was just getting started."

His third woman passes her hand over the sharp creases of his khaki pants and shirt, catches her image in his polished black shoes, peeks through his expensive camera, and photographs him crossing his eyes, twisting up his lips, putting on the red coat. He shows her his back and for a moment she is speechless.

"You know what it says?"

"Sure," she says. "I read English good."

"Okay. What's it say?"

She pauses. "Say you want me to stay with you tonight."

All that day she tells him exaggerated stories of an American giant who kills great cats with his teeth and cooks weeping men on a spit.

"Hasn't met me yet," the Corporal says.

She speaks of voodoo, curses, magic things. She moves over him, works on him, looks between her thighs. "You sick?"

The Corporal is ashamed.

"No worry," she says. "I get you someone. You be cured plenty quick."

A hot whisper of an afternoon breeze pushes at the drapes. He is openmouthed, open-eyed, seeing only his important red coat.

The Corporal winces at the stink but allows her to pull him around a corner. She drops his right hand as she ducks into a shop. He stoops at a window and looks in at her short legs and the high slit of her purple dress. Above him are rows of plucked birds strung by the neck, spinning slowly in the wind, and skinned, pop-eyed rabbits hung in a sprint; nearby are iron tanks of green eels, tripe, water snakes, gutted fish. There is an aquarium where squid throw out their bundle of arms and glide down to a darker corner. Here the men dress in baggy shorts, squat openly in the streets, scurry as though they have boys on their backs. Gray smoke twists up from pot stoves placed outside the doorways.

The prostitute comes out, showing her gapped teeth as she smiles, a wet, paper-wrapped package in her hands. "You cure," she says.

The Corporal expects her to give him the package, but instead the prostitute hands it to a heap of rags that is abruptly next to him, rocking from foot to foot. Her hair is like wax, her upper lip is darkly mustached, her long nails corkscrew from her fingers.

"Witch," the prostitute says.

The witch rips off the papers, chews into a squirming carp, finds the pulsing heart with her fingers, pops it in her mouth. Her fingers mull around in the entrails. She wipes her bumped face with the juice, and then raises up an eye patch to peer at the Corporal with a gray pupil. She seems surprised. "You the island man."

The Corporal turns for an explanation, but the prostitute has disappeared. When he turns back to the witch, only the carp is there, lying on paper on the street, its eye staring up with loathing.

The Corporal runs down the hotel corridor and hits his door hard. The door swings inward, banging the wall. His gold watch, his camera, his important red coat are gone.

* * *

Then the Corporal sees the American giant she'd been talking about. It is a bright Sunday morning, his last day of rest and relaxation. As he packs, he looks down to the street and sees the prostitute strolling with a sun-pinked man who is probably six feet eight inches tall. He is wearing a Panama hat and a yellow suit; he jauntily leans on a cane. The prostitute speaks and the American smiles, raising overjoyed eyes to the window. The American yells, "You!" and the Corporal steps away from the open window.

The Corporal jerks and jounces and pushes into the snapping canvas on highway curves. Across from him are two other replacements, a private and a helicopter pilot. The private is named Skeeter; the pilot Kenya. Skeeter operates a radio and appears to want to go deaf—he takes a toothpick out of his pocket and begins jabbing it into his ear.

The pilot will not speak. He merely stares with rowdy eyes when the Corporal talks to him. The big truck guns up a hill, changes gears, squeals as it stops. Road dust rolls in through the open back, and Kenya gets up, brushing his pants. He says, "You in a crazy company, boy. Your captain's the boogeyman."

Him. He is standing there with his pink head shaved, his great mustache waxed. Yes: six feet eight, maybe two hundred eighty pounds, and the boy's gold watch on his wrist. He peers at a clipboard and looks up after he reads their names. He recognizes the Corporal with a "Har!" He opens his powerful arms to the troops and smiles with deep pleasure at what he is preparing to say: "I'm Captain Saint Jones!"

Kenya whispers, "The boogeyman."

Captain St. Jones inspects the replacements and approves of all but the Corporal. "Look at you," he says, and touches the

Corporal's name patch. It is hanging by only a stitch. And his pants come uncreased at the Captain's notice, his polished boots look sandpapered, his zipper, of course, is undone.

Captain St. Jones scowls down. "You're not a soldier," he says. "You're a ragman."

Ragman. The Corporal feels hexed. He weakens. His underwear suddenly tatters, his collars fray, seams abruptly rip open, leaving spider legs of thread. He discovers yellow slugs in his boots, peels and rinds in his overnight pack, green mildew and sticky webs over everything. He pushes a cleaning rod down his M16 and pulls out steel that is striped with crawling ants.

And then the ragman gets an idea. At night he creeps into the Captain's tent and puts a finger on all the things in it, making them crack, cleave, spot with rust.

St. Jones throws up the flap of his tent in fury and peers at his company. The rising sun is big behind Captain St. Jones, and his men grow hunched at the sight of him. He wears a musketeer's plumed hat, high black boots are pulled up to his thighs, a great sword hangs at his side, and his spurs ring when he moves. "Okay, men. Have it your way." He dips his fingers in a jar and twists wax into his mustache. And then he grins. "Patrol!"

The Corporal is ordered to pack for the Captain. The rips in his blankets have been neatly patched, pants seams sewn, cracks in plastic cemented together, spots of rust polished out. When the tent is down, the great cot folded, the air mattress stamped flat, the Corporal discovers an old wooden trunk in the jungle close by. He wrenches open the catch and heaves up the lid. Inside are his expensive camera, his important red coat, the carp the witch had chewed open. The Corporal presses the coat to his cheek and passes his fingers lovingly over the green dragon.

The Corporal sits in the helicopter, his legs swinging in the wind, watching high grass spray away as they wobblingly lift off. Jungles sway under them, green and yellow birds dart and soar away. The open fields are gold and steamy and roll in the air blasts like cooking broth. They aren't gone twenty minutes before Kenya dips the helicopter to the right so St. Jones can point to weeds parting for stooped runners. He yells words that the Corporal cannot hear and then hangs by one arm from a strut, clenching his silver sword in his teeth. He jumps down and sprints into the jungle. High palms swoop away from him, great trees shake. The chopper cuts and sways and hammers the air over little people who are cowering helplessly in the weeds. One of them stands and picks his weapon up, but words are apparently spoken, for he stops and cocks his head to the left and is pulled down into the grass. Another stands and runs to the jungle, then is tripped and swallowed up. A painted man appears in a rain cape of weeds and angles a bazooka up at the chopper's guns when he is surprised by a big hand on his rope belt and disappears. Again and again it happens like that, and then Captain St. Jones gets up, waving his big arms overhead, wincing at the chopper's wake as it lowers to him. He jumps up into the helicopter and wipes the sword with his palm. He is panting a little but happy. The Captain grins at Kenya and Skeeter and the Corporal. "Here is greatness," says Captain St. Jones.

A journalist in green fatigues patrols with the company for a day, bellying through the yellow savannah, whispering into a tape recorder, snapping pictures of the geography, the plunder, the piled-up bodies. He takes a group portrait with Captain St. Jones eating grapes in a hammock, his patrol sitting cross-legged below him. And there will be a dark photograph, too, of a villager hung by his ankles from a high tree as Skeeter interrogates him.

"Getting anything from him?" the journalist asks.

"Nope," Skeeter says.

The Captain appears in his high boots and plumed hat and tells Skeeter to step aside. Gripping the sword with both hands, the Captain swipes it upward through the man's body. The skin bursts open with an explosion of green bats and straw. His blowing hair is grass. The journalist attempts a picture but the iris on his camera won't open. Skeeter looks sheepish. The Captain pats him on the cheek and says, "You were asking the wrong questions."

The Corporal spies a black shape in the woods.

On patrol, a soldier drops to his knees and slumps over. There are no apparent wounds in him, but his eyes roll up with death when he is lifted. Another soldier on patrol leaps into swamp water, pitching onto his sides and back as he slaps at the phantom fire that is creeping up to his ears. A private keeps on sleeping as his squad makes preparations. A buddy walks over to wake him up and finds a screwdriver hole in the private's throat. Green leeches suck all the blood from an overweight sergeant in one night. A private drowns on his canteen water even as he's drinking it. Cigarette packs are poisoned.

And they walk into a village of grass huts. A cooking fire of gray embers is in the center, with young boys around it, playing a game with their fingers. A pretty girl is stripped and appraised. Mothers are lined up with babies at their hips.

Skeeter interrogates them in their language and they give him poor inventions. Away in a steamy clearing, an old woman is singing in high pitch, "*Yo ti ya yam i no bi tamba co o no.*" As she approaches, the villagers get down on elbows and knees, praying, pitching away their coins, slapping themselves with open palms.

The Corporal is pulled to her. He can't explain it. And then he sees that she is rocking from foot to foot in gunnysacks and signaling that he ought to come nearer. Her hair is like wax, her upper lip darkly mustached. Only the eye patch is missing. She leers at the Corporal and her teeth are gray pebbles. She inchingly raises up her skirt.

The Corporal wakes up in moonlight with her body cold beneath him. He can't recall all that happened. One of his eyes has been poked out and the pain is enormous. He pushes himself up from the witch but somehow she holds him even in sleep. And then a smile comes to her lips and she simpers at the Corporal. "You mine now," she whispers and permits his escape from her. The Corporal is naked in a green swamp and his Army company has disappeared. His skin is painted with blood. He looks down to the witch in puzzlement and she opens a path to the west.

And now *he* is the boogeyman. The Corporal follows his company at a great distance. He can hear cassette players, helicopters, warning shots that rap the trees and provoke the monkeys into wild jabber. And he can pause and hear slippered footsteps behind him or pick out the stink of skunks killed on a highway, of forty fish belly-up in a pond. Spiders are in the grass she walks, a gray sickness powders the leaves, yellow slugs grow huge as legs and are overslow in eating the dogs they catch.

* * *

Horrible things happen to the Army company as they sleep. A man can wake up cloaked in white moths or with a mitten of red ants on his right hand. A pool they sip from on one night can become, by dawn, a dry cup in the earth heaped with poisonous frogs. Young men die of their nightmares or sleepwalk into the jungle. Skeeter, for example, is missing. And the moon is always green.

Even Captain St. Jones is ill with high fevers, headaches, muscle cramps that purple his legs. His ankles swell until his bootlaces pop, and stomach pains make him walk in a stoop. At last he sicks up a pale, gutted fish, its green gills pulsing, its eyes plucked out.

Her work.

The pygmies are in a circle, eating raw meat and rice from wooden bowls. Crossbows lie at their feet. They speak poetry in whispers, oil themselves, pat their skin with leaves. One of them presses another's wrist and points.

The Corporal stands in steep rock shadow, as still as he can.

The pygmies get to their feet, pick up their bows, and slowly creep back into the jungle. The Corporal sits in their places, collecting their body heat, their spoken words, their unspoken memories. Skeeter's bones are in a pit on gray coals. The Corporal strips off pieces of Skeeter's meat and eats them as the pygmies sing their word for *boogeyman.*

A deer yanks a leaf from a limb and swings her head to the south, staring into the jungle as she chews. Her ears perk up and she leaps away, but Captain St. Jones intercepts the doe on the path, wrapping his great arms around her neck and riding her down into a sprawl. The doe chops at the peat with her hooves and nearly wrenches away, but the Captain rips his bayonet up through the hide and pulls out the deer's insides. High up in the cavity, he pushes the Corporal's watch, his camera, and especially his important red coat.

How can he explain his hunger, his great yearning? The Corporal crashes wildly through the forest, crying with a voice not his own. He cuts his biceps and calves with a sharpened stick and paints the trees with his blood. At night, in anguish, he yowls for her and, as a sign of his misery, chips out his teeth with rocks.

He makes traps for the soldiers—straw pits, rope nooses, bamboo spears. He pushes spotted leopards into their camps. When the company is out on patrol, he rips apart packs and boxes and tents, looking for his possessions. The Corporal despairs of ever getting them back, of the witch ever letting him go.

Captain St. Jones and his company are caught, up to their mouths in swamp water, their weapons high overhead in the moonlight. A picket fence of water-spray spurts up from machine-gun fire as the soldiers drop to the swamp bottom or plunge over into high reeds and cattails. Cartridges jam, gun actions go rigid, hand grenades fly wildly awry. Her work. Captain St. Jones pulls himself up from the swamp, cautiously rolls onto a path, and limpingly sprints away.

He is jogging through jungle many hours later when one leg gets caught in a vine and Kenya spins crazily over the cow path, a rope looped around his right arm and neck. The skin has been peeled from his face.

Here there is peace. Here, in the swamp, there are no signs of the Captain or his patrol. The Corporal sleeps on green moss that is dappled with sunlight. He opens his mouth for rainwater. Canaries sing, deer forage daintily, monkeys screech and trapeze in the treetops, a parrot nibbles at a peanut the Corporal pinches between his fingertips.

St. Jones stops to read his compass and then slaps reeds aside to push to the east. And then, yes, the putrid smell. He presses more rapidly toward it and drops to his knees by the evil body of the deer. He swipes away horseflies and jams his hand into a soup of maggots. Withers collapse at his pressure, a snake pours itself out of the open mouth. And then Captain St. Jones owns them again: the gold watch, the expensive camera, and the important red coat. He wraps his great arms around them and rolls happily on the ground.

Around the swamp, the native people make a pole corral and, with spades and dams and nightwork, a deep moat that all hope will keep the boogeyman in. Ceremonies are performed on the banks opposite his camping place. In them the one-eyed boogeyman emerges from the jungle, painted in blood, in a rain cape of weeds, and a witch doctor's hand is placed on the heads of pretty maidens until the boogeyman agrees on one. And then the girl is weighted with stones and guided into the creek water as mothers pray that the green army and the boogeyman will stay away from their village.

A helicopter passes overhead, and the Captain rushes out into the burning open, swooping his arms up, crying for help, pitching rocks at its underbelly as it yaws and speeds away. He goes back to the elephant and eats with the jackals until his belly aches, and then he scoops up his possessions, wiping his mouth on the lettering of the silk coat. The Captain perceives a greater darkness and looks up at the sun. Only a slice of it is apparent as the moon nears eclipse.

His sign. The Captain looks for a parrot and sees one in a treetop to the west. He wrenches his way through weeds and high grass until he comes upon green water and a pole corral. He splashes deeply into the creek and then dips underwater to pass his hands over the shapes of pretty girls lolling among the carp and eels, crab traps of stones at their hips. The green water irons out over him, and then he bursts up from the bottom, blowing air, and raises up his sword. "Yes!" shouts Captain St. Jones.

Hush. There the giant is, sleeping, his huge back rounded, the great sword at his side, glinting silver light. The Corporal spies his worshiped coat, the powerful lettering, the green dragon and the golden torch of its breath. He slides into the creek from his island and swims across underwater, coming up with a gasp when he strokes into a holy girl and her leg oozes away.

And yet the Captain sleeps. The Corporal creeps up onto the hot sand and attempts to pick up the coat. He can't budge it—the weight is like an iron car, or as though the earth's gravity has been changed just for it. The Corporal slinks closer and clasps the great sword, then jumps up in the increasing darkness and hacks at the Captain's head, splitting it from crown to ear.

One roar of pain and the Corporal knows he has killed a giant bear. St. Jones is laughing at the Corporal's ignorance as he swaggers out of the jungle, the gold watch on his wrist, the expensive camera strapped around his neck. "Caught me sleeping, did you, boy? Only wish I got a snapshot of you to send it to your witch." The Captain easily picks up the coat and painstakingly brushes away the sand. "And now you can give me the sword."

"You'll kill me," the Corporal says.

The Captain glimpses something on the island and snaps his fingers. "Quickly."

And then there is night in the late afternoon. The moon overtakes the sun and all is still. Jungle animals cower, the green waters cease, and the Corporal swings the great sword overhead with a strength that is more than his own. He hears a wild howl as the blade cuts through jungle air, and then he hears the Captain scream with agony as his hot blood splashes over the Corporal, as the earth pounds with his great collapse.

And then light seeps down through the treetops and the witch is stooping over Captain St. Jones, unstrapping the camera, working the gold watch off his wrist, pressing her nose into the all-important red coat. Caws and screeches and yipes rise up from the island as she rapidly zips on the coat and pulls the corpse into green water that swallows up the Captain. His body grows black with eels.

The Corporal had expected a metamorphosis once the coat was put on, but the witch is no prettier, no more appealing, and just as poor as she's always been. She keeps patting the material and peering at herself in the water, so pleased with herself that she can pay little attention to the Corporal as he swims back to his island in a downpour.

The Corporal wears a green uniform and an eye patch when he appears on the opposite bank. The native people speak in whispers, and when the Corporal looks up, they hear the wopping noise and the high whine of an engine. The pretty girls are taken away and the witch doctor makes a ceremony of wiping off his paint. The Corporal sits there patiently, awaiting the helicopter's approach, the peace accords, another place.

True Romance

The supernatural — the constant, unstated threat is that the creature will kill the baby

The first-person narrator — she does tell us how she feels + expose her vulnerability as a nursing mother, but also the fierceness/protectiveness of this state.

What other currents of tension are operating in the story? + True Romances + currents of tension set up + developed.

?

It was still night out and my husband was shaving at the kitchen sink so he could hear the morning farm report and I was peeling bacon into the skillet. I hardly slept a wink with Gina acting up, and that croupy cough of hers. I must've walked five miles. Half of Ivan's face was hanging in the circle mirror, the razor was scraping the soap from his cheek, and pigs weren't dollaring like they ought to. And that was when the phone rang and it was Annette, my very best friend, giving me the woeful news.

Ivan squeaked his thumb on the glass to spy the temperature—still cold—then wiped his face with a paper towel, staring at me with puzzlement as I made known my shock and surprise. I took the phone away from my ear and said, "Honey? Something's killed one of the cows!"

He rushed over to the phone and got to talking to Annette's husband, Slick. Slick saw it coming from work—Slick's mainly on night shift; the Caterpillar plant. Our section of the county is on a party line: the snoops were getting their usual earful. I turned out the fire under the skillet. His appetite would be spoiled. Ivan and Slick went over the same ground again; I poured coffee and sugar and stirred a spoon around in a cup, just as blue as I could be, and when Ivan hung up, I handed the cup to him.

He said, "I could almost understand it if they took the meat, but Slick says it looks like it was just plain ripped apart."

I walked the telephone back to the living room and switched on every single light. Ivan wasn't saying anything. I opened my robe and gave Gina the left nipple, which wasn't so standing-out and sore, and I sat in the big chair under a shawl. I got the feeling that eyes were on me.

Ivan stood in the doorway in his underpants and Nebraska sweatshirt, looking just like he did in high school. I said, "I'm just sick about the cow."

He said, "You pay your bills, you try and live simple, you pray to the Lord for guidance, but Satan can still find a loophole, can't he? He'll trip you up every time."

"Just the idea of it is giving me the willies," I said.

Ivan put his coffee cup on the floor and snapped on his gray coveralls. He sat against the high chair. "I guess I'll give the sheriff a call and then go look at the damage."

"I want to go with you, okay?"

The man from the rendering plant swerved a winch truck up the pasture until the swinging chain cradle was over the cow. His tires skidded green swipes on grass that was otherwise white with frost. I scrunched up in the pickup with the heater going to beat the band and Gina asleep on the seat. Ivan slumped in the sheriff's car and swore out a complaint. The man from the rendering plant threw some hydraulic levers and the engine revved to unspool some cable, making the cradle clang against the bumper.

I'd never seen the fields so pretty in March. Every acre was green winter wheat or plowed earth or sandhills the color of camels. The lagoon was as black and sleek as a grand piano.

Gina squinched her face up and then discovered a knuckle to chew as the truck engine raced again; and when the renderer hoisted the cow up, a whole stream of stuff poured out of her and dumped on the ground like boots. I slaughtered one or two in my time. I could tell which organs were missing.

Ivan made his weary way up the hill on grass that was greasy with blood, then squatted to look at footprints that were all walked over by cattle. The man from the plant said something and Ivan said something back, calling him Dale, and then Ivan slammed the pickup door behind him. He wiped the fog from inside the windshield with his softball cap. "You didn't bring coffee, did you?"

I shook my head as he blew on his fingers. He asked, "What good are ya, then?" but he was smiling. He said, "I'm glad our insurance is paid up."

"I'm just sick about it," I said.

Ivan put the truck in gear and drove it past the feeding cattle, giving them a look-over. "I gotta get my sugar beets in."

I thought: the cow's heart, and the female things.

Around noon Annette came over in Slick's Trans Am and we ate pecan rolls hot from the oven as she got the romance magazines out of her grocery bag and began reading me the really good stories. Gina played on the carpet next to my chair. You have to watch the little booger every second because she'll put in her mouth what most people wouldn't step on. Annette was four months pregnant but it hardly showed—just the top snap of her jeans was undone—and I was full of uncertainty about the outcome. Our daytime visits give us the opportunity to speak candidly about things like miscarriages or the ways in which we are ironing out our problems with our husbands, but on this occasion Annette was giggling about some goofy woman who couldn't figure out why marriage turned good men into monsters, and I got the ugly feeling that I was being looked at by a Peeping Tom.

undercurrent

Annette put the magazine in her lap and rapidly flipped pages to get to the part where the story was continued, and I gingerly picked Gina up and, without saying a peep to Annette, walked across the carpet and spun around. Annette giggled again and said, "Do you suppose this actually happened?" and I said yes, pulling my little girl tight against me. Annette said, "Doesn't she just crack you *up?*" and I just kept peering out the window. I couldn't stop myself.

That night I took another stroll around the property and then poured diet cola into a glass at the kitchen sink, satisfying my thirst. I could see the light of the sixty-watt bulb in the barn, and the cows standing up to the fence and rubbing their throats and chins. The wire gets shaggy with the stuff; looks just like orange doll hair. Ivan got on the intercom and his voice was puny, like it was trapped in a paper cup. "Come on out and help me, will you, Riva?"

"Right out," is what I said.

I tucked another blanket around Gina in the baby crib and clomped outside in Ivan's rubber boots. They jingled as I crossed the barnyard. The cattle stared at me. One of the steers got up on a lady and triumphed for a while, but she walked away and he dropped. My flashlight speared whenever I bumped it.

Ivan was kneeling on straw, shoving his arm in a rubber glove. An alarm clock was on the sill. His softball cap was off, and his long brown hair was flying wild as he squatted beside the side-laying cow. Her tail whisked a board, so he tied it to her leg with twine. She was swollen wide with the calf. My husband reached up inside her and the cow lifted her head indignantly, then settled down and chewed her tongue. Ivan said, "P.U., cow! You stink!" He was in her up to his biceps, seemed like.

"You going to cut her?"

He shook his head as he snagged the glove off and plunked it down in a water bucket. "Dang calf's kaput!" He glared at his medicine box and said, "How many is that? Four out of eight? I might as well give it up."

I swayed the flashlight beam along the barn. Window. Apron. Pitchfork. Rope. Lug wrench. Sickle. Baling wire. And another four-paned window that was so streaked with pigeon goop it might as well've been slats. But it was there that the light caught a glint of an eye and my heart stopped. I stepped closer to persuade myself it wasn't just an apparition, and what I saw abruptly disappeared.

Ivan ground the tractor ignition and got the thing going, then raced it backward into the barn, not shutting the engine down but slapping it out of gear and hopping down to the ground. He said, "Swing that flashlight down on this cow's contraption, will ya, Riva?" and there was some messy tugging and wrestling as he yanked the calf 's legs out and attached them to the tractor hitch with wire. He jumped up to the spring seat and jerked into granny, creeping forward with his gaze on the cow. She groaned with agony and more leg appeared and then the shut-eyed calf head. My husband crawled the tractor forward more and the calf came out in a surge. I suctioned gunk out of its throat with a bulb syringe and squirted it into the straw but the calf didn't quiver or pant; she was patient as meat and her tongue spilled onto the paint tarp.

Ivan scowled and sank to his knees by the calf. The mother cow struggled up and sniffed the calf and began licking off its nose in the way she'd been taught, but even she gave up in a second or two and hung her head low with grief.

"Do you know what killed it?"

Ivan just gaped and said, "You explain it." He got up and plunged his arms into the water bucket. He smeared water on his face.

I crouched down and saw that the calf was somehow split open and all her insides were pulled out.

After the sheriff and the man from the rendering plant paid their visits, the night was just about shot. Ivan completed his cold-weather chores, upsetting the cattle with his earliness, and I pored over Annette's romance magazines, gaining support from each disappointment.

Ivan and I got some sleep and even Gina cooperated by being good as can be. Ivan arose at noon but he was cranky and understandably depressed about our calamities, so I switched off *All My Children* and suggested we go over to Slick's place and wake him up and party.

Annette saw I was out of sorts right away, and she generously agreed to make our supper. She could see through me like glass. At two we watched *General Hospital*, which was getting crazier by the week according to Annette—she thought they'd be off in outer space next, but I said they were just keeping up with this wild and woolly world we live in. Once our story was over, we made a pork roast and boiled potatoes with chives and garlic butter, which proved to be a big hit. Our husbands worked through the remaining light of day, crawling over Slick's farm machinery, each with wrenches in his pockets and grease on his skin like war paint.

Annette said, "You're doing all right for yourself, aren't you, Riva."

"I could say the same for you, you know."

Here I ought to explain that Annette went steady with Ivan in our sophomore year, and I suspect she's always regretted giving him to me. If I'm any judge of character, her thoughts were on that subject as we stood at the counter and Slick and Ivan came in for supper and cleaned up in the washroom that's off the kitchen. Annette then had the gall to say, "Slick and me are going through what you and Ivan were a couple of months ago."

Oh no you're not! I wanted to say, but I didn't even give her the courtesy of a reply.

"You got everything straightened out, though, didn't you?"

I said, "Our problems were a blessing in disguise."

"I know exactly what you mean," she said.

"Our marriage is as full of love and vitality as any girl could wish for."

Her eyes were even a little misty. "I'm so happy for you, Riva!"

And she was; you could tell she wasn't pretending like she was during some of our rocky spots in the past.

Slick dipped his tongue in a spoon that he lifted from a saucepan and went out of his way to compliment Annette—unlike at least one husband I could mention. Ivan pushed down the spring gizmo on the toaster and got the feeling back in his fingers by working them over the toaster slots. My husband said in that put-down way of his, "Slick was saying it could be UFOs."

"I got an open mind on the subject," said Slick, and Ivan did his snickering thing.

I asked if we could please change the topic of conversation to something a little more pleasant.

Ivan gave me his angry smile. "Such as what? Relationships?"

Slick and Annette were in rare form that night, but Ivan was pretty much of a poop until Slick gave him a number. Ivan bogarted the joint and Slick rolled up another, and by the time Annette and I got the dishes into the sink, the men were swapping a roach on the living-room floor and tooling Gina's playthings around. Annette opened the newspaper to the place that showed which dopey program was on the TV that evening. Slick asked if Ivan planted the marijuana seeds he gave us and Ivan shrugged. Which meant no. Slick commenced tickling Annette. She scooched back against the sofa and fought him off, slapping at his paws and pleading for help. She screamed, "Slick! You're gonna make me pee on myself!"

Ivan clicked through the channels but he was so stoned all he could say was, "What *is* that?"

Annette giggled but got out, "*Creature from the Black Lagoon!*"

I plopped Gina on top of her daddy's stomach and passed around a roach that was pinched with a hairpin. I asked Ivan, "Are you really ripped?" and Ivan shrugged. Which meant yes.

The movie was a real shot in the arm for our crew. My husband rested his pestered head in my lap and I rearranged his long hair. There was a close-up of the creature and I got such a case of the stares from looking at it you'd think I was making a photograph.

Ivan shifted to frown at me. "How come you're not saying anything?"

And I could only reply, "I'm just really ripped."

Days passed without event, and I could persuade myself that the creature had gone off to greener pastures. However, one evening when Ivan was attending a meeting of the parish council, my consternation only grew stronger. Gina and I got home from the grocery store and I parked the pickup close by the feed lot so I could hear if she squalled as I was forking out silage. Hunger was making the cattle ornery. They straggled over and jostled each other, resting their long jaws on each other's shoulders, bawling *mom* in the night. The calves lurched and stared as I closed the gate behind me. I collared my face from the cold and as I was getting into the truck, a cry like you hear at a slaughterhouse flew up from the lagoon.

I thought, I ought to ignore it, or I ought to go to the phone, but I figured what I really ought to do is make certain that I was seeing everything right, that I wasn't making things up.

Famous last words!

I snuggled Gina in the baby crib and went out along the pasture road, looking at the eight-o'clock night that was closing in all around me. I glided down over a hill and a stray calf flung its tail in my headlights as its tiny mind chugged through its options. A yard away its mother was on her side and swollen up big as two hay bales. I got out into the spring cold and inspected the cow even though I knew she was a goner, and then I looked at the woods and the moonlighted lagoon and I could make out just enough of a blacker image to put two and two together and see that it was the creature dragging cow guts through the grass.

The gun rack only carried fishing rods on it, but there was an angel-food-cake knife wedged behind the pickup's toolbox, and that was what I took with me on my quest, my scalp prickling with fright and goosebumps on every inch of me. The chill was mean, like you'd slapped your hand against gravel. The wind seemed to gnaw at the trees. You're making it up, I kept praying, and when I approached the lagoon and saw nothing, I was pleased and full of hope.

The phone rang many times the next day, but I wouldn't get up to answer it. I stayed in the room upstairs, hugging a pillow like a body, aching for the beginning of some other life, like a girl in a Rosemary Rogers book. Once again Annette provided an escape from my doldrums by speeding over in the orange Trans Am—her concern for me and her eternal spunk are always a great boost for my spirits.

I washed up and went outside with Gina, and Annette said, "What on earth is wrong with your phone?"

I only said, "I was hoping you'd come over," and Annette slammed the car door. She hugged me like a girlfriend and the plastic over the porch screens popped. The wind was making mincemeat of the open garbage can. And yet we sat outside on the porch steps with some of Slick's dope rolled in Zig-Zag papers. I zipped Gina into a parka with the wind so blustery. She was trying to walk. She'd throw her arms out and buck ahead a step or two and then plump down hard on her butt. The marijuana wasn't rolled tight enough and the paper was sticking all the time to my lip. I looked at the barn, the silo, the road, seeing nothing of the creature, seeing only my husband urging the tractor up out of a ditch with Slick straddling the gangplow's hookups and hoses. Slick's a master at hydraulics. The plow swung wide and banged as Ivan established his right to the road, then he shifted the throttle up and mud flew from the tires. One gloved hand rested on a fender lamp and he looked past me to our daughter, scowling and acting put out, then they turned into the yard and Annette waved. Ivan lifted his right index finger just a tad, his greeting, then turned the steering wheel hand over hand, bouncing high in the spring seat as Slick clung on for dear life.

Annette said, "My baby isn't Ivan's, you know."

I guess I sighed with the remembering of those painful times.

Annette said, "I'm glad we were able to stay friends."

"Me too," I said, and I scooched out to see my little girl with an angel-food-cake knife in her hands, waddling over to me. "Gina!" I yelled. "You little snot! Where'd you get that?"

She gave it to me and wiped her hands on her coat. "Dut," Gina said, and though my husband would probably have reprimanded her, I knelt down and told her how she mustn't play with knives and what a good girl she was to bring it right to me. She didn't listen for very long, and I put the knife in my sweater pocket for the time being.

Annette was looking peculiar, and I could tell she wanted an explanation, but then there was a commotion in the cattle pen and we looked to where Ivan and Slick were pushing cow rumps aside in order to get close to the trough. They glared at something on the ground out there, and I glanced at the cake knife again, seeing the unmistakable signs of blood.

"I'm going out to the cattle pen," I imparted. "You keep Gina with you."

Annette said, "I hope your stock is okay."

The day was on the wane as I proceeded across the yard and onto the cow path inside the pen, the cake knife gripped in my right hand within my sweater pocket. The cattle were rubbing against the fence and ignorantly surging toward the silage in the feed trough. Slick was saying, "You oughta get a photograph, Ivan." My husband kept his eyes on one spot, his gloved hands on his hips, his left boot experimenting by moving something I couldn't see.

I got the cattle to part by tilting against them with all my weight. They were heavy as Cadillacs. And I made my toilsome way to my husband's side only to be greeted with a look of ill tidings and with an inquiry that was to justify all my grim forebodings. He asked, "Do you know how it happened, Riva?"

I regarded ground that was soggy with blood and saw the green creature that I'd so fervently prayed was long gone. He was lying on his scaly back and his yellow eyes were glowering as if the being were still enraged over the many stabbings into his heart. Death had been good for his general attractiveness, glossing over his many physical flaws and giving him a childlike quality that tugged at my sympathy.

Again Ivan nudged the being with his boot, acting like it was no more than a cow, and asking me with great dismay, "How'd the dang thing get killed, do ya think?"

And I said, "Love. Love killed it. Love as sharp as a knife."

Slick gazed upon me strangely, and my husband looked at me with grief as I sank to the earth among the cattle, feeling the warmth of their breathing. I knew then that the anguish I'd experienced over those past many months was going to disappear, and that my life, over which I'd despaired for so long, was going to keep changing and improving with each minute of the day.

Sleepless

She walked her house by day, discovering it. She sat on the rough wooden staircase to the basement in order to look at the singing orange light of the gas water heater. She used a letter opener and stripped up a cattail of gray wallpaper in order to know how the front parlor was back when white folks occupied the room without speaking and sent their hard eyes down the newspaper and percolated their nasty opinions. She sashayed along the upstairs hallway, from the yellow sewing room past the second bedroom with the pretty girl-things in it, the hidden clothes hamper that sent your dirty laundry down a tin drop to the washer and dryer, the pink, wallpapered bedroom that was hers and Claude's and into the ugly, turquoise bathroom with the iron eagle-claw tub and the bleary green view of the yard. She would peer into the spotted mirror over the sink but could only see herself. She would trail her own fingers along the fingerprinted walls but get no history from them. Her family had been moving into the old house for four days before she knew about the wickedness in it, but that was like hearsay or a butterfly of gossip that Avis overheard in the yellow room. She could make out seventy years of ordinariness downstairs, but it was like the upstairs had been soaped clean, like the evil memories had been painted over, the conversation interrupted.

* * *

Avis predicted a girl for a pregnant woman in Gretna, and that there would be no complications. She guessed, but didn't say, that the woman was twenty-eight or so, a Cancer, husband worked with his hands. Avis got a pledge of five dollars from her but knew she could forget about ever seeing it. Husband would say, "You *what?*" And that would be that. One of her weekly people complained that Avis had moved without giving him her new telephone number. She apologized but said she would have recommended his standing pat in the options market, anyway; she wasn't getting great signals. Avis told a white woman in Papillon to get a second opinion before going ahead with the hip surgery. She'd come up with twenty for Avis, probably mail it in a card with pink begonias on the cover, and inside the card she'd write, "Your prophecies have helped so many!" Claude phoned to get the numbers at noon, but Avis only saw a zero and nine and her husband said maybe he'd skip the play. She got a crank call from the Nebraska chapter of the white supremacists. A pregnant girl at Mercy High School wouldn't say why she was calling, only that she had a big problem and needed Mrs. Walker's advice. Avis suggested the girl say nothing to her parents just yet, that the problem was going to be ironed out in a week or two. The girl promised her a hundred dollars but Avis said, "You keep it, honey."

Her four-year-old scuttled in from the green screened porch, singing out that they'd gotten their first mail, and Avis opened the striped film processor's envelope in order to see the color prints she'd had made to promote herself: a jolly, overweight, sorta-pretty woman with cocoa-brown skin and lavender eyes and maybe an excess of jewelry. "You like me in these, Lorna?"

The little girl said yes.

Avis wasn't sure. She supported herself on the pantry

countertop and pored over each snapshot, but could only exclude the garden one with the jagged light along her neck. Her ten-year-old came in from the pantry room with a box of cups and saucers that were wrapped in tissue paper. Avis turned a slightly overglamorous photograph toward her older daughter and asked, "You like this one, Priscilla?"

Priscilla cut through the box's strapping tape with a paring knife as she scowled at the photograph. "Give you the likeness of a fish."

Avis saw what she meant. "You sure are plainspoken."

She clipped out an Omaha *World-Herald* newspaper coupon and printed out the classified ad she wanted inserted in the personals: "Anxiety—Questions—Curious? PSYCHIC READINGS, Mrs. Walker." She went to the telephone to read the new number strip and there was another call. She guessed it was from Bellevue. Offutt Air Force Base. White man saying, "You the psychic?"

Avis thought he was probably in his fifties, possibly a widower, sandpaper in his deep voice, nights misspent in a workingman's bar, and sleeping with a girl many years younger. He ought to stop it. She said, "You want to hear my advice or your prospects?"

He coughed out a laugh and said, "You tell me."

Her secret impressions were that he wanted a new occupation. Hated his job. Could be an Air Force sergeant getting near retirement. She could see a green shirt. She could smell gasoline. Avis pressed the receiver between her ear and shoulder, put a notepad on the pantry countertop, shoved six bracelets up from her wrist. "You know a lot about engine parts," she said. "You want to open a shop?"

She heard him light a cigarette. "Go on."

"I see some problems scraping up the money, you know?

You're thinking about some government insurance, you got a notion to take your cash out? Keep your money in there, you hear? And maybe you ought to get some more on-the-job experience before you jump into this." Avis was cartooning on the notepad, a boy with big eyes and hanging arms, his head angled over to the right. She said, "You can't jump into owning a motor-repair shop with just your pension."

She was getting more certain as the guy sighed cigarette smoke away from his phone and said, "You still got my attention."

Avis covered her eyes with one palm and interpreted all she was picking up. "Okay. I am perceiving a whole lotta pain. Your wife, she's older, and she maybe had some bad operation in the hospital and stayed poorly from it? Also, there's this sweet young girl coming into your house to sorta take care of your missus and clean up and so on. And you, you been creeping down to her room, *nightly,* saying please, sugar, please, please, please, and just once more and such. You know what I'm talking about. A pretty young thing. She's a nurse? You ought to stop it. Evil things could happen."

"Hate to say it, but you're way off in left field."

Avis asked, "Has your wife passed away?"

"Nope. She's right here, sipping her java."

"Huh." Avis could see a dayroom and his urgent body and the girl's legs high and snugging him in. And she could see another room and a gray-haired woman asleep, or dying, purple flowers arranged all around her.

Her caller said she was right about the shop idea and the insurance policy, but then she'd gone off on a tangent.

"We don't usually mess up like this," Avis said.

"I know that," the sergeant said. "The wife had her palm read by you at that psychic fair in South Omaha. She got me to believing you were accurate as radar."

Avis said she was sorry and that she must've been picking up impressions from another person close by. She explained that it was simply like getting a couple of overlapping stations at one spot on a radio; or like when you snapped one picture on top of another and came up with a double exposure.

"Had days like that myself."

After he'd hung up, Avis peered at her notepad until she knew what was missing. And where the boy's head angled over to the right, she penciled in a rope and a noose.

She was up late, sewing draperies and slipping the pink-tuliped chintz onto rods for Claude to put up in the morning. Everything was jumbled from moving in, nothing was in its place; even the twin bed in the sewing room was just iron springs on a pinewood frame. She stitched a drapery hem and snipped the thread at the machine's presser foot. She could hear Claude tramping up the staircase and stopping to look in on the girls. And then she heard him creak open the door to the sewing room and peer in without a word as she stooped over her plastic bobbin case. Without looking up, Avis said, "You awake too?"

She could hear his slow pant but Claude was apparently just staring at her as she picked through spools of navy blue and black in search of a simple dark green. She asked, "How you like the pink?" but Claude said nothing. He could have been an onlooker at a grisly street accident, or a jazzed-up boy who'd put a coin in the slot to gape at her body in a peep show.

Avis asked, "You okay?" and turned; but the sewing-room door was already touching shut. And then she saw a deep red paint abruptly spray over the wallpaper and haltingly trickle down and little by little disappear. And when she smelled the penny odor of blood, she knew she'd had an inspiration of evil in the past.

* * *

Avis placed the flat of a knife on a garlic clove and pounded it hard with her fist. She peeled away the dry husk and then chopped the pink garlic toe inside, faintly singing as she dumped the choppings into a bowl. The girls were at the dining-room table, saying silly things and giggling as they drew with crayons on a split-open grocery sack.

Yard pictures in the windowpanes were warped and slurred by rain. Claude was sitting outside in his Parks and Recreation Department truck, waiting for the rain to pass, the radio probably tuned to a Royals game. He looked at his new property and lit a second cigarette. Gray smoke tumbled against the window glass. He tipped his cap down over his eyes and appeared to nap.

She could hear the girls arguing over the red crayon. The more Lorna yelled for it, the more Priscilla ignored her. Avis looked at the recipe and spooned oregano into the bowl, then went into the dining room, drying her hands on a paper towel. Lorna was crying. Avis said, "Just give her the red, Priscilla."

"She always hogs it!"

"How long have *you* had it?"

"All day!" Lorna said.

Avis looked down at the big house her girls had crayoned on the grocery-bag paper. One upper room contained the huge round heads and scarecrow bodies that meant human beings to Lorna. Priscilla was completing work on a sickroom. A yellow-haired boy was axing an overweight woman who was hooked up to orange tubes and green hoses. Huge amounts of blood were springing from her belly in raindrops and petals of red.

"Yuck, Priscilla."

"Momma, it's a story."

"Whose story?"

Priscilla kept the red crayon in her lap as she worked on the yellow-haired boy.

"Are you listening, Priscilla? Who's the boy killing?"

Lorna looked at her sister's picture and said, "The momma!"

Avis crouched by her younger daughter and put a finger under a girl who had brown sticks for legs. The girl's wrists joined around the green coveralls of a white man with jack-strawed hair. "And who's this, Lorna?"

Lorna screwed up her face as she looked at the brown girl in the picture, then smiled with accomplishment. "She the bitch!"

"How'd you learn that word, Lorna?"

Lorna squirmed a little.

"Priscilla?"

Priscilla snickered and Avis said, "You want to get slapped, you keep it up."

Claude pushed open the yard door and stamped the rain off. Lorna jumped from her chair and leapt into her daddy's arms. He picked her up overhead and kissed her knees and let her drop to his belly. "Saberhagen got hisself another win," Claude said.

Avis couldn't stop pressing. "How do you know the story, Priscilla?"

The girl wouldn't speak. She was as psychic as Avis, as skeptical as Claude. Her mother thought she'd lose her second sight pretty soon and happily accept just being ordinary. Claude sauntered around to look at the picture and complicate everything by saying, "You *good*, baby girl! You got talent! You know she could draw like that, Avis?"

Avis asked, "How's the story come out?"

Priscilla got a stupid look as she peered out at the yard. Avis presumed she was seeing it played out, but only like a creepy late-night movie on their black-and-white television. Priscilla glanced down at her picture again and said, "The girl gets killed."

"You get pictures in your head?"

"Sorta."

"She get killed by the person called her a bitch?"

Priscilla didn't say.

"Who kills her?"

Her husband whispered into Lorna's ear, "Your momma and sista makin' their spook talk again." The telephone was ringing, so Claude carried his little girl into the pantry room to get it.

Avis tilted up Priscilla's chin and squinted into the girl's angry brown eyes. "Who kills her?"

"The boy."

"A boy you know?"

The girl jerked her chin away. "You're *pestering* me!"

Claude stood in the doorway with Lorna. "Telephone must be for you. Won't speak to me."

Avis said, "How do you know the story, Priscilla?"

"I don't know how I know! I just do!"

Avis hugged the girl and angled her head low enough to smell her slightly dirty hair. She said, "I know, sweetheart. I know." And then she went to the telephone.

"Can't sleep."

"And you are?"

"I'll try, but I keep getting scared."

His speech was poky, like he was sickly or a little simple, gloom or ignorance in his voice, a sulky white boy in some Omaha high school. His problem would wind up being about a pretty girl who liked him less than spit. "Could you give me your name?"

"Gary."

Sixteen, probably skinny, poor, obnoxious. She could hear him playing with the phone cord, and then there was an overlong pause.

Avis said, "I like your name."

He didn't say anything.

"How old are you, Gary?"

He gave it some thought and said, "Twenty-eight."

"You lying to Avis?"

The boy seemed irked and scared. His right hand was possibly squeezed between his thighs, tendering himself. "Sixteen and twelve is twenty-eight, isn't it?"

She couldn't follow that talk, so she only said, "You sound younger."

Gary said, "Each night it's the same."

"Well, upsetting dreams do repeat themselves."

"I'll be standing outside this big house, and then I'll be standing inside it. And I walk into the rooms."

"And why is that scary?"

The sleepless boy didn't speak.

Avis said, "Just tell me what you see."

"Just the rooms and some people."

"You mean, people you know?"

He didn't say.

"How do they react toward you?"

"Afraid."

"And why is that?"

She heard nothing.

"Hello?"

Priscilla was in an apron and cranking an opener around a can of tomato paste. Without looking up, she asked, "Is he still on the phone?"

"Are you there?"

Gary sighed. "I just wish I could sleep."

"I know." She jotted *Willa* on the notepad.

"Could you help me sleep?"

"I'll try."

Priscilla tipped the can and spooned the tomato paste into a bowl.

Gary asked, "Is she your daughter?" and then, as if he'd overstepped, Gary hung up the phone.

She attempted to get a promotional interview at an Omaha weekly newspaper and was introduced to a Scorpio named Ed who admitted to writing "hash and thumbsucker pieces" that he could probably fit her story into. She could smell his prejudice like onions as his yellow eyes skirted away from hers and cigarette ash dripped onto his notebook and she was cornered and misinterpreted and preposterous words were put in her mouth. She heard herself saying she could predict a baby's sex from skin temperature. She got a sick feeling whenever she got too close to a Ouija board. Auras were usually pineapple-colored. She said a psychic was someone who saw the world just like an educated person could see the word *dear,* say, in *read.* She said she'd get herself into an altered state between consciousness and sleep and house ghosts and spirits would grayly appear in the corner of her eye.

"And you talk to them?"

"Yes."

"In English?"

She didn't say.

Ed showed his tan teeth in a skeptical smile. "I take it, then, you're sort of a spook psychiatrist."

Avis said, "I try to route them toward the God-spirit to seek peace and love."

"You ever get laughed at when you say that?"

She scowled in an august and sovereign way. "I have been brought to test by ugliness of all kinds."

Ed jotted a note and then cagily thought for a second or two, tapping his thin lips with his pen. "And how would you describe this God-spirit?"

She said, "The Holy Trinity of the Father, Son, and Comforter, plus the twelve high spirits that help govern the universe."

Ed hurriedly scratched his pen across his notepad and shook his head in rich amusement. "Avis, you're almost too good to be true."

She took the 30th Street bus to Ames and walked up Larimore Avenue with groceries from the Safeway, getting winded as the street tilted up, and watching curtains part as scornful widows frowned out at her. An old Austrian in a cardigan sweater was weakly scratching a garden rake across his bluegrass lawn just east of her place, and she could see him tilting against the upright rake and angrily judging her skin and attitude. Everyone white on the block was sickly and old and scared about how much they could get for their properties now that the colored were moving in. Four homes were just recently for sale. The Walker house was white, two stories high, with a green screened porch and a great, sick elm in the yard, and halfway up the slope of Larimore, at exactly the spot where boys had to stand hard on their bicycle pedals in order to try the hill.

Avis couldn't go another step with her heavy groceries, so she put the sack on the sidewalk and angled across the yard with just the spoiling things until she got the sense she was being stared at from her own house. Her purple eyes went upstairs to the sewing room and to a joyless girl of eighteen in a yellow

Priscilla seems unaware of having been inhabited (?) by the ghost — if that's what happened

nightgown sitting there at the windowsill with her jaw in her brown right hand. And then, as though she'd been ordered elsewhere, the girl turned aside and slowly withdrew, anxiously tying the nightgown strings over significant breasts. And half a minute later Priscilla was greeting her on the green screened porch in her own slippers and an overlarge yellow nightgown that she got from her mother's closet.

"Were you upstairs?" Avis asked.

The girl said yes, she'd been sick.

"You know why you're wearing my nightgown?" she asked, and Priscilla considered herself with surprise.

Avis couldn't sleep, so she went down to the front parlor to work. She paper-clipped a snapshot to her press release and slipped in a note about her willingness to appear without fee, and then she printed the addresses of Omaha television and radio stations on some manila envelopes. Cold air passed over her and she got up to close the kitchen door. And then she had a premonition. She looked into the pantry room and just then the telephone rang.

She picked up the receiver, and Gary was already speaking. "A great big white house and green trees. A ceiling light on in an upstairs window, and I'm on the sidewalk looking up as some woman in an overcoat—she's a doctor, I think—she's moving the drapes aside. And then I'm inside the house on the upper floor. And I know the people there."

"Are they your family?"

"She passed away."

"Your mother?"

"She was in a lot of pain. And she passed away and it was easier for her."

"Is it your mother you see?"

Quiet. She could practically see him. His green eyes were squinched up, stopping his tears; his open mouth was twisted with pain. She skipped ahead by asking, "How about your father?"

Gary governed himself a little and said, "Dad was just coming in from the night shift."

"Was?"

"You know, night shift? Overtime?"

"Just then you talked like you weren't actually dreaming."

Gary didn't say anything.

"And then what happens?"

Gary said bitterly, "As if you actually wanted to hear."

"Only if this is helping."

He sighed. "Another room and this colored girl is sleeping on a cot. No. She's not sleeping, she's *pretending* to sleep. Her back is to me. And I lie down next to her and she's hot for it. She knows what she wants and so do I. And one thing leads to another and I'm touching her, and then she spoils it. She speaks. Her speaking is how I wake up."

"You recognize her?"

"She's not the girl. She's changed. She says angry things."

"Angry things?"

He gave that some thought before saying, "I mean, things that make me angry."

"You keep calling it a nightmare."

"Uh-huh."

"How come you're scared?"

He paused before replying. "It's how I look when I get up from the bed, the bed where the girl was sleeping. My jeans and sweatshirt are soaked with blood. You can hear it dripping onto my shoes, and there's a pool of blood on the carpet. And I've got an ax in my hand."

"Have you hurt somebody?" Avis asked.

"How do you mean?"

"Is this a nightmare, or are you telling me something you've done?"

"A nightmare."

"You're sure you know the difference?"

He didn't answer.

"Have you been in prison, Gary?"

"You could say that."

"You out now?"

"At night."

She ignored that; she thought he was trying for petty mystery by being intentionally vague. "You said she speaks, the sleeping woman. Could you tell me what she says?"

"Don't know." She could hear him becoming more passive, pitying himself. His voice was like that of a punished child.

"Here's something you can try, Gary. Next time you get your nightmare, just look at your hand. You right-handed?"

"Yes."

"Okay. Look at your right hand. You'll get power over your nightmare. You'll get rid of those people and you'll sleep. Could you try that?"

Gary wasn't paying attention. She could imagine his green eyes wildly straying, his lewd hand petting himself as he said, "I could try a lot of things with you."

She sighed. "You're getting into trash talk now."

"You think you could handle it?"

"Just be yourself, Gary." She could hear nothing but quiet for such a long time that Avis said, "Are you there?"

And then she had an overpowering feeling that she wasn't alone downstairs, that his sleeplessness was phony, his night call a trick, that she was only being set up for harassment or rape,

Avis has a vision? But it's too palpable for that— of Gary in her room molesting her

and a white boy who called himself Gary was creeping toward her even then. She heard his footsteps on the dining-room carpet, heard the soft bump and rasp of a wooden chair being slightly brushed by his jeans, but she was too frightened to turn. Her skin prickled and her heart trip-hammered, but she was otherwise stymied, her own body shrinking inside itself. She couldn't scream or run upstairs or even release the telephone from her ear. She smelled an overindulgence in Old Spice cologne and heard Gary say over the phone, "She's you." And then his cold palms cupped her large breasts as though weighing them and, in his ignorance of women, crushed them painfully in his caress. Her legs mellowed and she nearly collapsed, but Gary lunged against her, holding her against the doorjamb as his chill lips skipped over her short hair in pecks, and she heard him whisper, "In my nightmare. She's a girl I know. And then she's you."

Avis could only hang up the telephone, and with that his hard pressure eased up, his kiss disappeared. She spun around and the room was empty. Even the Old Spice fragrance was gone. And then the telephone was ringing again and she wept until it stopped.

His nightmare became hers, and she saw herself walking through a big house at night. Cold wallpaper on her fingertips, the steps yawping as she went upstairs, fragrant rose bath salts in the air, a strip of light beneath one door, a girl singing along with The Temptations, and when Avis opened the door, an hour had passed and there was a pool of blood on milk-white bed linens and on the floor the horrible, hacked-apart body of a pretty young nurse. Her skin a cocoa brown.

Avis jerked up and pressed her racing heart with her hands as she placed herself in her own room, her nail polish on top of the dresser, the old, deep chair in the right spot, Claude's coveralls in a heap, and Claude piled up like railroad ties beside her.

She couldn't sleep. Avis looked in on the girls, pulling a green blanket up on Lorna, and then she went down to turn the gas up under a teapot. She got back all she could of the nightmare and again recognized her feelings as she looked at the young nurse's good body: jealousy, loathing, sexual passion. *She ought to be for me.*

She got a cup as the hot water piped and then stooped over with a pain in her side that wasn't her own. Her pain was a needle, then a spike, and the pain opened up wider than her own hips, and Avis dropped to the floor. His mother. She clasped her pelvis, crossing her arms. "Hush," she said, and the pain was only a soreness, and then the soreness passed.

Avis opened her eyes and reached to the kitchen countertop to pull herself up. "You poor old woman," she said.

Claude sipped his coffee as Avis scrambled eggs for him in a measuring cup. A light mist grayed the morning. The yellow eggs sputtered when she poured them into the skillet. Claude said, "Could be a prank, you know. Could be white people want us outa here. Niggers movin' in, wreckin' the neighborhood."

"Isn't just the phone calls, Claude."

"Except you been havin' days you seen right and days you seen wrong. You ain't at a hunnert percent yet. You could be messin' up."

Avis told a Creighton University professor to spend more time around water, but to look out for a Pisces who was intent on injuring his reputation. A Fremont woman said she wanted to give up smoking, but Avis said the problem wasn't cigarettes, it was her marriage. And she was bullying her husband. Avis got a card from the elderly woman in Papillon, with pink begonias on the cover and a crisp twenty-dollar bill inside. And she got a call from a talk-show host, saying he'd like Avis to join him next month on his *Coffee Break* radio program.

Six or more times per day the telephone would ring, and no one would speak when Claude or Lorna said hello. Avis presumed that was Gary. She got in touch with the Nebraska State Department of Corrections, but an uppity secretary said she couldn't talk about ex-prisoners to just anybody who happened to call. She once woke up, and Claude wasn't Claude but a whiskeyed crazy man lying on a dirty bed, his skin very pale, his haunted green eyes wide open, his mechanic's hands clamped over his ears in order to stop the tramping noise of footsteps on the stairway. When the door opened, the apparition disappeared and Claude walked inside in his pajamas. "Went for a water glass," Claude said.

Then, one night when she was getting out of her slip, Avis looked at the pink flowers on the chintz draperies and imagined a great mahogany bed angled under the high window. She could see a gray-haired woman sleeping, a purple tube up her nose and her hands greenly wormed with veins. Avis could hear an oxygen tank lightly hissing as a mechanic in green coveralls knocked sneakily at the sewing-room door, sandpaper in his voice as he harshly whispered, "Willa!"

Avis went up to the girls' room and gently tugged Lorna's right thumb from her mouth. She walked over to the twin bed alongside the wall, but Priscilla was sitting up in her nightgown, her right elbow on the windowsill and her jaw in her hand, solemnly contemplating the yard as if she were trying to interpret words that were not being spoken aloud. Avis rapped sharply on the window glass, and Priscilla's dark eyes jumped with shock before she simpered and said, "Hi, Momma."

"Whatta you up to?"

"I just couldn't sleep."

Avis inchingly touched a curtain aside and gazed down. No one was there. "You playing me for a fool?"

Priscilla hopped up into her bed and snickered as she covered her face with a pillow.

She'd given Claude some numbers, and he'd used them on the greyhounds in Sioux City, winning four hundred and sixty dollars on a quiniela. Claude learned about it from one of the brothers on the job the next morning and was still joyous when he called Avis from the Fontenelle Park golf course, where they were laying in irrigation pipe. Claude said his supervisor might just let him off early so he could bring home a big celebration. And then he said his cheeseburger was on the hot plate, kissed the mouthpiece, and said good-bye.

Avis heard the clank of the mailbox lid and waited for Lorna to carry it in until she recalled that she was in kindergarten now. And Priscilla would be in the public-school cafeteria, probably not eating, and swapping her cupcakes for change. Avis went out and collected two bills, a letter from a cancer patient in Soldier, Iowa, and a dirty envelope from the weekly newspaper with the name Ed Cziraki crudely printed on the upper-left corner in red ink. She sat down on the porch steps and scooped out some yellowed newspaper photographs from twelve years ago. Wording had been jaggedly torn away from the pictures, but she could make out what looked like "mercy killing" below a snapshot of a big mahogany bed and a sick woman's body, nicely arranged beneath a darkly stained sheet. Another newspaper picture was copied from a high-school yearbook. A joyless boy with yellow hair in an ugly paisley shirt, his hard eyes half an inch too close to his nose and his nose a half an inch too long. She thought, Who's the ferret? And then knew. Gary. The last photograph was of a pretty black girl who'd been hacked apart with an ax. Written over the picture was "Your household haints, I s'pose."

Avis put the clippings back inside the dirty envelope and shoved it deep in her apron pocket and pulled herself up heavily on the handrail. Eyes were on her as she walked inside and indignantly locked the door.

She tried to nap on the sofa in the parlor but couldn't sleep for the upsetting visions of Gary twelve years ago, a slaughterhouse ax in his reddened hands, his clothes sagging heavily with blood and the blood plipping like nickels onto the carpet.

Avis got up and paid her bills, cleaned up the parlor, then emptied the wastepaper baskets into a green plastic bag and dragged it out to the garbage cans in the cinder alley. The day had lost twenty degrees since noon and indigo rain clouds were turtling in. She had a premonition and looked up at the upstairs rooms of her house and at the high windows that Claude had covered with plastic weatherproofing and tape. She pulled her overcoat closed and looked up the alley at a gray old woman clipping her hedges in a see-through raincoat, her black poodle standing between her legs and idly sniffing the air.

She thought, Everything's changed. And she thought, Don't go back, but she did. She walked to the stoop and peered through the windowpanes of her kitchen door and saw the big house as it was when white people lived in it. Aprons and sweaters were hanging from nails, and green rubber boots made tan by yard mud had been slung into a corner. A twelve-year-old Knights of Columbus calendar was tacked up in the pantry, and hooked over the top of the inner door was a rubber-tipped cane.

Avis yelled unreasonably, "Hello?" and paused a second

before stepping inside. She walked into the kitchen and called again, "Hello?" She could see the pecan pie she'd made on the stove top, and Lorna's storybooks by the telephone, but she could also make out a rickety table with a checkered plastic tablecloth and on it salt and pepper cellars and a soup bowl of truck-stop matchbooks. She opened cabinets and found her own soups and stews and cereal boxes, but also their ill-matched assortment of cups and plates, potato chips, beef jerky, whiskeys, antacids, cough syrups, and a huge variety of pills. Avis bumped against her own purple sofa in the parlor but only saw a heap of magazines and a frayed green chair no more than two feet away from a round-tube Zenith television. Unwashed clothing was on their sofa, overalls were on the floor, a motor was in pieces on an open newspaper.

She was getting overlapping stations at one spot on the radio. She was apparently picking up impressions from another person close by.

And then she went upstairs to the evil past, with apprehension, even chill panic, but also with pity and reverence and the concern of a physician. She could see photographs stair-stepped up the wall: of a young sailor in Navy whites standing with a testy older woman in a tulle wedding dress; a baby boy in cowboy boots in the yard with a 1956 Plymouth; the boy in a blue Cub Scout uniform; and Gary now fourteen years old, at Christmastime, getting a shotgun from his father. And at the top of the stairs was Willa—not a snapshot but an apparition, a girl acting out scenes from the past. Willa just stepping out of the bathtub and prettily reaching up for a towel in the hallway closet as green eyes spied on her nakedness. And Willa in a terry-cloth robe, carrying a food tray, slightly smiling at someone Avis couldn't see. And yet again Willa, in nurse's whites, standing up against the clothes hamper and shutting her eyes with pleasure as she yielded her right breast to Gary's father. Engine grease from his night shift was under his fingernails. Avis could smell gasoline on his green coveralls. And then the hallway was empty.

Avis saw a strip of light beneath the closed door to her bedroom. She put her palms to the door and perceived the room as she'd imagined it days ago, the great mahogany bed underneath the high window, the oxygen tank in the corner, the gray-haired woman sinking into a heap of yellowed pillows under stained patchwork quilts as an orange rubber tube drained into a saucepan. When Avis opened the door, the woman's head lolled fragilely to the right and she gazed at Avis for many seconds before saying weakly, "Gary?"

His mother was the first.

Avis shut the door and walked down the hallway to the second bedroom. Her girls' room; now a boy's. His orange window shades were down, rumpled airplane sheets were on the bed, jeans were hanging over a chair. Atop a small study desk were a black telephone, high-school geometry and physics textbooks, a German beer stein of pencils and pens, and a green rubber triceratops. Everything preserved as it was twelve years ago—the overhead light was always on, and the program on the big console radio was always at high volume.

She withdrew to the only other upstairs room. Her sewing room. Willa's room. Her own mattress had been rolled up and kept in place in the corner with a clothesline rope, but Willa's mattress was on the iron springs of a pinewood cot just like her own, and the pressed bed linens were sprinkled with cheap perfume. Except for some hangers covered in tissue paper, Avis's closet was empty, but Willa's was deep in nurse's whites and party clothes and seven pairs of shoes. A striped rug was oddly placed on the floorboards in order to cover up the pink stain of spilled fingernail polish.

Avis was surprised at how little else she could pick up in the room; there was only a teaspoon of history in it. She fractionally parted her drapes, as if that were just another orderly step in a mechanical process, and she peered out without passion or emotion as she slipped her heavy overcoat off and let it pour onto her sewing bench. She sat on her own spare bed and then slumped over on the iron springs with her right palm tightly clamped to her purple eyes so she could put all the scenes and pictures together.

Rain pattered against the window glass and gradually increased in power and then it was as hard and gray and vertical as upright piano wire. Avis heard the porch door open and seconds passed and then the porch door closed again. She yelled down, "Priscilla?" and then she heard a heavy tramping up the steps, and she got another horrible glimpse of that night twelve years ago: In the big walk-in closet where her girls' pretty things were now, Gary sagged among his jeans and paisley shirts and calf-high motorcycle boots, a pop-eyed boy with a pink tongue squeezed out of his mouth, his purpled head jutted to the right by an angled towrope and noose.

And now she could hear him opening his mother's bedroom door, and seconds passed and Gary repeated her killing, his right hand raising up high overhead and slashing down, his left palm up to shield his eyes from the hot spray of blood. Gary was probably hearing over and over again the hard, squelching slugs of the ax and his mother's dying groans of pain, but Avis only heard stillness, and then she heard the boy open the second bedroom door and yank the towrope down from his tie rack, and then, with an angry second thought, Gary shut that door too.

Hairs stood up on her arms and neck, goose bumps pebbled her skin like a rain on a nighted pond, but Avis stayed as she was. His footsteps approached the yellow sewing room, Willa's room, and as the door creaked open, the penny odor of blood and the sink upsurge of corruption were so overpowering that Avis pinched her nose, but she couldn't move in spite of her understanding of what his sleeplessness was and what Gary had meant by being in prison. The iron springs dipped with Gary's added weight, and the springs rang a little as the boy rolled into her and nudged his hard sex between her thighs. His clothes were soaked with the hot blood of more than one body and he stank like a cat rotting in the street. His hand painted her skin red with blood as Gary gingerly touched her cheek and petted back her hair and said "Willa!" raspily, just as his father did. And Avis at last found the voice to say, "It's time to go to sleep, Gary."

The boy paused and then avidly pressed his lips to her ear in a kiss that was cold as an apple slice. He placed his heavy ax on top of her hip, and Avis could feel its sharp pressure through her skirt as the boy's hand sought her breast. And she could feel his crazy hate and jealousy as Gary again pushed into her, saying, "You want it and you know it."

Avis took his hand in a motherly way and said, "Gary, please. Don't hate anymore. Give up. Go to sleep. You're a ghost."

And then she could feel a slight change in him, and Gary was lying on his back, acknowledging her words. She turned, and Gary was just a sickly boy in a paisley shirt, his green eyes windowpaned with tears. Avis said, "Everybody's forgotten," and she heard the iron springs ease up as his nightmare slowly ended and, at last, Gary slept.

Red-Letter Days

JAN 25. Etta still poorly but up and around. Hard winds all day. Hawk was talking. Helped with kitchen cleanup then shop work on Squeegee's fairway woods. Still playing the Haigs I talked him into in 1963. Worth plenty now. Walked up to post office for Etta's stamps. $11.00! Went to library for William Rhenquist's book on Court and Ben Hogan's *Five Lessons.* Finest golf instructions ever written. Will go over with Wild Bill, one lesson per week. Weary upon return. Skin raw. Etta said to put some cream on. Didn't. We sat in the parlor until nine, Etta with her crossword puzzles, me with snapshots of Wild Bill at junior invitational. Will point out his shoe plant and slot at the top.

FEB 2. Will be an early spring, according to the groundhog. Went ice fishing on Niobrara with Henry. Weren't close as boys but everybody else dying off. Extreme cold. Snaggle hooks and stink bait. Felix W on heart and lung machines and going downhill in a handcart. Dwight's boy DWI in Lincoln. Sam Cornish handling trial. Would've been my choice too. Aches and pains discussed. Agriculture and commodities market and Senior Pro/Am in August. Toughed it out till noon—no luck with catfish—then hot coffee at Why Not? Upbraided for my snide comments about *The People's Court.* Everyone talking about Judge Wapner the way they used to gush about FDR. Wild Bill's poppa slipped into the booth and hemmed and hawed before asking had *William* said anything to me about colleges. You know how boys are. Won't talk to the old man. Writing to Ohio State coach soon re: sixth place in Midwestern Junior following runner-up in Nebraska championship. And still a sophomore! Etta tried for the umpteenth time to feed me haddock this evening. Went where it usually does.

FEB 9. Hardly twenty degrees last night. Felix W's funeral today. Walked to Holy Sepulchre for the Mass, then to cemetery; taking a second to look at our plots. Hate to think about it, but I'll have my three score and ten soon. Felix two years younger. Estate papers now with Donlan & Upshaw. (?!) Widow will have to count her fingers after the settlement. Etta stacked her pennies in wrappers while watching soaps on television. Annoying to hear that pap, but happy for her company. And just when I was wishing that kids and grandkids would have been part of the bargain, Wild Bill showed up! And with his poppa's company car, so he took us out to the golf club and we practiced his one and two irons from the Sandhills patio, hitting water balls I raked up from the hazards in September. Wild Bill in golf shoes and quarterback sweats and Colorado ski sweaters, me in my gray parka and rubber overboots. You talking *cold?* Wow! Wild Bill getting more and more like Jack Nicklaus at sixteen. Lankier but just as long. His one irons reaching the green at #2! And with a good tight pattern in the snow, like shotgun pellets puncturing white paper. Homer and Crisp stopped by to hoot and golly, say how amazing the kid is, but I wouldn't let em open their traps. The goofs. W. B.'s hands got to stinging—like hitting rocks, he said—so we quit. Have spent the night perusing *Reader's Digest.* Our president making the right decisions. Feet still aching. Hope it's not frostbite.

* * *

FEB 20. Helped Etta with laundry. Hung up sheets by myself. Brrr! Heard Etta yelling "Cecil!" over and over again, nagging me with instructions. Would not look back to house. We're on the outs today. Walked the six blocks to Main for the groceries ($34.17!) and got caught out in the snow right next to liquor store. Woman I knew from a Chapter Eleven took me home. Embarrassing because I couldn't get her name right. Verna? Vivian? Another widow. Says she still misses husband, night and day. Has the screaming meemies now and again. Was going to invite her inside but thought better of it. In mailbox the *Creighton Law Review* and *Golf Digest,* plus a jolly letter from Vance and Dorothy in Yuma, saying the Winnebago was increasing their "togetherness." A chilling prospect for most couples I know. Worked in shop putting new handgrips on Henry's irons. Eighteen-year-old MacGregors. Wrong club for a guy his age, but Henry's too proud to play Lites. Work will pay for groceries, just about. Half pint of whiskey behind paint cans. Looked and looked and looked at it; took it up to Etta. Ate tunafish casserole—we appear to be shying away from red meat—and sat in parlor with magazines. Tom Watson's instructions good as always but plays too recklessly. Heard he's a Democrat. Shows. Etta's been watching her programs since seven. Will turn set off soon and put out our water glasses as the night is on the wane and we are getting tired.

MAR 4. Four inches last night and another batch during the day. Old Man Winter back with a vengeance. Woke up to harsh scrape of county snowplows. Worried the mail would not get through, but right on the button, including Social Security checks! Helped Etta put her Notary Sojack on, then trudged up to the Farmer's National. Whew! Kept a sawbuck for the week's pocket money. Hamburger and coffee at the Why Not? Happy to see Tish so chipper after all her ordeals. Checked out Phil Rodger's instruction book from library—great short game for Wild Bill to look at, although Lew Worsham and Paul Runyan still tops in that category. Helped Etta tidy up. Wearing my Turnberry sweater inside with it so cold, but Etta likes the windows open a crack. Shoes need polishing. Will do tomorrow or next day. Early to bed.

MAR 12. Etta has been scheming with Henry's wife about retirement communities in Arizona. And where would our friends be? Nebraska. We put a halt to that litigation in September, I thought. Expect it will be an annual thing now. Dishes. Vacuumed. Emptied trash. Hint of spring in the air but no robins yet. Wild Bill lying low, sad to say. Girlfriend? Took a straw broom into rooms and swatted down cobwebs. Etta looking at me the whole time without saying a word. Haircut, just to pass the time. Dwight snipping the air these days, just to keep me in his chair. We avoided talk of his boy and jail. Seniors potluck meeting in Sandhills clubhouse at six. Shots of me with Dow Finsterwald, Mike Souchak, Jerry Barber still up in the pro shop. Worried new management would change things. (Pete Torrance still my idea of a great club professional.) And speaking of, a good deal of talk about our own Harlan "Butch" Polivka skunking out at Doral Ryder Open and the Honda Classic. Enjoyed saying I told you so. We'll plant spruce trees on right side of #11 teebox, hoping to make it a true par five. Alas, greens fees to go to six dollars (up from 50¢ in 1940) and Senior Pro/Am will have to go by the way this year. Hours of donnybrook and hurt feelings on that score, but Eugene late in getting commitments. Everybody regretting August vote now. Would likes of Bob Toski or Orville Moody say no soap to a $1,000 appearance fee? We'll never know. Betsy said it best at Xmas party. Eugene looks very bad, by the by. Chemotherapy took his hair, and a yellow cast to his eyes now. Wearing sunglasses even indoors. Zack much improved after operation. Wilma just not all there anymore. Etta tried to make coherent conversation but got nowhere. Sigh. Upon getting home, wrote out checks to water and sewer and Nebraska power and so on, but couldn't get checkbook to zero out with latest Farmer's National statement. Frustrating. Sign of old age, I guess. Will try again tomorrow.

MAR 17. Looked up Wild Bill's high-school transcript. Would appear he's been getting plenty of sleep. We'll have to forget about Stanford and the Eastern schools and plug away at the Big Eight and Big Ten. Etta wearing green all day in honor of old Eire. Was surprised when I pointed out that Saint Patrick was English. Told her that *Erin go bragh* joke. She immediately telephoned Betsy. Late in the day I got on the horn to Wild Bill, but Cal said he was at some party. Kept me on the line in order to explore my opinions on whether Wild Bill ought to get some coaching from the Butcher, acquire some college-player techniques. Well, I counted to ten and took a deep breath and then patiently, patiently told old Cal that golf techniques have changed not one iota in sixty years and that Harlan "Butch" Polivka is a "handsy" player. Lanny Wadkins type. Hits at the golf ball like he was playing squash. Whereas I've taught Wild Bill like Jack Grout taught Nicklaus. Hands hardly there. And did Cal really want his boy around a guy known to have worn knickers? Well, old Cal soothed my pin feathers some by saying it was only a stray notion off the top of his head, and it was Cecil says this and Cecil says that since his son was ten years old. Told *him* that *Erin go bragh* joke. Heard it, he said. From Marie.

* * *

MAR 20. Took a morning telephone call for Etta, one of those magazine-subscription people. Enjoyed the conversation. Signed up for *Good Housekeeping.* Weather warming up at last, so went out for constitutional. Wrangled some at the Why Not? Squeegee getting heart pains but don't you dare talk to him about his cigarettes! Lucky thing Tish got between us. She says Squeegee still doesn't know what to do with his time; just hand-washes his Rambler every day and looks out at the yard. Encouraged her talk about a birthday party for Etta with the girls from the Altar Sodality and the old "Roman Hruska for Senator" campaign. Ate grilled cheese sandwich in Etta's room. Did not blow it and broach party subject. Etta's hair in disarray. We sang "The Bells of St. Mary's" and "Sweet Adeline" while I gave it a hundred strokes. Etta still beautiful in spite of illness. Expressed my sentiments.

MAR 25. Worked out compromise with insurance company. Have been feeling rotten the past few days. Weak, achy, sort of tipsy when I stand up. Hope no one stops by. Especially Wild Bill. Sandhills' one and only PGA golf professional is again favoring us with his presence in the clubhouse. Will play dumb and ask *Harlan* about his sickly day at the Hertz Bay Hill Classic. Etta's temperature gauge says it's fifty-two degrees outside; March again going out like a lamb. Ike biography petered out toward the end. Haven't been able to sleep, so I took a putter from the closet and have been hitting balls across the parlor carpet and into my upended water glass. *Tock, rum, rum, plonk.*

APR 1. Hard rains but mail came like clockwork. Nice chat with carrier. (Woman!) Quick on the uptake. April Fool's jokes, etc. Letters to occupant, assorted bills, and then, lo and behold, government checks. Wadded up junk mail and dropped it in circular file, then Etta walked with me to Farmer's. Enjoys rain as much as ever, but arthritis acting up some. Hefty balance in savings account thanx to Uncle Sam, but no pup anymore. One hospital stay could wipe us out. Have that to think about every day now as 70 looms on the horizon. Will be playing nine tomorrow with Zack, Mel, and Dr. Gerald S. Bergstrom, P.C. Hoping for another Nassau with old P.C. Lousy when "pressed," and the simoleons will come in handy. Evening supper with *Reader's Digest* open under milk glass and salad bowl. National Defense called to task. Entire Navy sitting ducks. Worrisome.

APR 4. Have put new spikes in six pairs of shoes now; at $15 a crack. Wrist is sore but easy money. Dull day otherwise. Walked over to Eugene's and played cribbage until five. Eugene is painting his house again. Etta and I have been counting and think this is the sixth time since Eugene put the kibosh on his housepainting business. You know he's retired because he will *not* do anyone else's house. Have given up trying to figure Eugene. Walked past Ben's Bar & Grill on the way home. Just waved.

APR 10. Wonderful golf day. Timothy grass getting high in the roughs, but songbirds out, womanly shapes to the sandhills up north, cattails swaying under the zephyrs, great white clouds arranging themselves in the sky like sofas in the Montgomery Ward. Homer and Crisp played nine with me and zigzagged along in their putt-putt. Hijinks, of course. Exploding golf ball, Mulligans, naughty tees. (Hate to see cowboy hats on the links. We ought to have a rule.) Even par after six, then the 153-yard par three. Hit it fat! Chopped up a divot the size of Sinatra's toupee and squirted the pill all of twenty yards. Sheesh! Examined position. Easy lie and uphill approach. Eight iron would have got me there ten years ago, but I have given in to my age. Went over my five swing keys and thought "Oily," just like Sam Snead. Hard seven iron with just enough cut to tail right and quit. Kicked backwards on the green and then trickled down the swale to wind up two feet from the cup. Homer and Crisp three-putted as per usual—paid no attention to my teaching—and I took my sweet time tapping in. *Quod erat demonstrandum.* Crisp says Butch has been claiming he shot a 62 here last July but, conveniently, with some Wake Forest pals who were visiting. Funny he never gets up a game with me. Tax returns in. Have overpaid $212, according to my pencil. Early supper, then helped Etta strip paint from doorjambs. Hard job but getting to be duck soup with practice. Will be sore tomorrow.

APR 15. Squeegee passed away just about sunup. Heart attack. Etta with Mildred as I write this. The guy had been complaining of soreness in his back but no other signs of ill health other than his hacking and coughing. Looking at yesterday's diary entry, I spot my comment on his "hitching," and it peeves me that I could not have written down some remarks about how much his friendship meant to me over these past sixty-five years. Honest, hardworking, proud, letter-of-the-law sort of guy. Teetotaler. Excellent putter under pressure. Would not give up the cigarettes. Will keep pleasant memories of him from yesterday, say a few words at the service. Weather nippy. Wanted booze all day.

APR 17. S. Quentin German consigned to his grave. Especially liked the reading from Isaiah: "Justice shall be the band around his waist, and faithfulness a belt upon his hips. Then the wolf shall be a guest of the lamb, and the leopard shall lie down with the kid; the calf and the young lion shall browse together, with a little child to guide them." And then something about a lion eating hay like the ox. Excellent applications to old age/erosion of powers/nature's winnowing process. Following, there was a nice reception at the Why Not? Haven't seen Greta since she had her little girl. Mildred wisely giving Squeegee's Haigs to the golf team at William Jennings Bryan. Etta and I took short constitutional at nightfall. Warm. Heather and sagebrush in the air. Have begun Herbert Hoover biography. Iowa boy. Engineer. History will judge him more kindly than contemporaries did. Low today; no pep.

APR 20. Etta sixty-seven. Took a lovely little breakfast to her in bed, with one yellow rose in the vase. Nightgown and slippers just perfect, she says. Foursome with Sam Cornish, Henry, and Zack. Shot pitiful. Kept getting the Katzenjammers up on the teebox. Hooked into the Arkwright rangeland on #3. Angus cattle just stared at me: Who's the nitwit? And then skulled a nine iron approach on #17 and my brand-spanking-new Titleist skipped into the water hazard. *Kerplunk.* Hate the expense more than the penalty stroke. And to top it off, Cornish approached me in pro shop with a problem on the Waikowski codicil. Hadn't the slightest idea what he was talking about. Sam has always loved those *ipse dixit*s and *sic passim*s, but that wasn't the problem. The problem is me. I just can't listen fast enough. Everything gets scrambled. I say to him, "What's your opinion?" And when he tells me, I pretend complete agreement, Sam pretends I helped out. Humiliating. Roosevelt at Yalta. Etta had her party today. She hadn't predicted it, so apparently I managed to keep the cat in the bag for once. Had a real nice time; plenty of chat and canasta. She needed the pick-me-up.

APR 25. Walked a slow nine with Henry and Eugene. No birdies, two bogeys, holed out once from a sand trap. Eugene and Henry getting straighter from the tees. Haven't pointed out to them that their mechanics haven't improved—they're just too weak to put spin on the golf ball these days. Lunched at Sandhills and shot the breeze until four, then walked by the practice range. Wild Bill out there with you know who. And Wild Bill slicing! shanking! Everything going right. Lunging at the ball like Walter Hagen. Butch dumbfounded. Addled. Looked at hands, stance, angle of club face, completely overlooking the problem. Head. Yours truly walked up without a word, put a golf ball on the tee, took a hard hold of Wild Bill's girl-killer locks and said, "You go ahead and swing." Hurt him like crazy. About twenty hairs yanked out in my hand. I said, "You keep that head in place and you won't get so onion-eyed." I just kept holding on and pretty soon those little white pills were riding along the telegraph wire, and rising up for extra yardage just when you thought they'd hang on the wind and drop. Walked away with Wild Bill winking his thanx and our kid pro at last working up the gumption to say, "Good lesson." Will sleep happy tonight.

APR 30. I puttered around the house until ten when Wild Bill invited me to a round with Wilbur Gustafson's middle boy, Keith. We've let bygones be bygones. Keith also on golf team. Ugly swing—hodgepodge of Lee Trevino and Charlie Owens—but gets it out okay. Keith says he hasn't got *William*'s (!) touch from forty yards and in, but scored some great sand saves. Was surprised to hear I lawyered. And Wild Bill says, "What? You think he was a *caddy?*" Was asked how come I gave up my practice, but pretended I didn't hear. Was asked again and replied that a perfectionist cannot put up with mistakes. Especially his own. Hit every green in regulation on the front nine, but the back jumped up and bit me. Old Sol nice and bright until one P.M., and then a mackerel sky got things sort of fuzzy. (Cataracts? Hope not.) Well: on #12, Wild Bill couldn't get the yardage right, so without thinking I told him, "Just get out your mashie." You guessed it: "What's a mashie?" And then we were going through the whole bag from brassie to niblick. Kids got a big kick out of it. Hung around and ate a hot dog with Etta, Roberta, and Betsy, then jawed with Crisp on the putting green. Watched as a greenskeeper strolled from the machine shed, tucking his shirt in his pants. Woman walked out about two minutes later. Won't mention any names.

MAY 6. Weather getting hotter. Will pay Wild Bill to mow yard. ($5 enough?) Endorsed government check and sent to Farmer's with deposit slip. Helped Etta wash and tidy up. Have been bumping into things. Match play with Zack, a one-stroke handicap per hole. Halved the par threes, but his game fell apart otherwise. Would have taken $14 bucks from him but urged Zack to go double or nothing on a six-footer at #18 and yanked it just enough. Zack's scraping by just like we all are. AA meeting, then Etta's noodles and meat sauce for dinner. (According to dictionary, P. Stroganoff a 19th century Russian count and diplomat. Must be a good story there.) Early sleep.

MAY 15. Nice day. Shot a 76. Every fairway and fourteen greens in regulation. Four three-putts spelled the difference. Took four Andrew Jacksons from Dr. Bergstrom, but ol P.C. probably makes that in twenty minutes. Will stop playing me for cash pretty soon. Tish got a hole-in-one at the 125-yard par three! Have telephoned the *Press-Citizen.* Her snapshot now in pro shop. Oozy rain in the afternoon. Worked on Pete Upshaw's irons until four P.M. His temper hasn't improved. Went to Concord Inn—Ettta driving—for the prime-rib special. Half price before six. And then out to Sandhills for Seniors meeting. We *finally* gave out prizes for achievements at Amelia Island tournament. (Marie sorry for tardiness, but no excuse.) Joke gifts and reach-me-downs, but some great things too. Expected our "golf professional" to give me a chipper or yardage finder, something fuddy-duddy and rank amateur, but the guy came through with a seven wood, one of those nifty presents you don't know you want until you actually get it. We have no agreement, only a truce. Zack got a funny Norman Rockwell print of some skinny kids with hickory sticks arguing golf rules on a green. Looked exactly like Zack and Felix and Squeegee and me way back in the twenties. Talked about old times. We're thinking Pinehurst for next winter trip. Have suggested we open it up to get some *mannerly* high-school golfers to join us. (Would be a nice graduation present for Wild Bill.) Everybody home by nine.

MAY 22. Early Mass and then put in an hour mixing up flapjack batter at the Men's Club pancake breakfast. Heard Wilma has Alzheimer's. Earl Yonnert having thyroid out. Whole town getting old. Went out to links at noon. Wild Bill there by the green with his shag bag, chipping range balls into a snug group that looked just like a honeycomb. Etta asked him to join us. Have to shut my eyes when she gets up to the ball, but she skitters it along the fairway okay. Wild Bill patient, as always. Has been getting great feelers from Ohio State, thanx to my aggressive letter campaign and his Nebraska state championship. Everything may depend upon his ranking on the Rolex All-American team. Says he hopes I'll visit him in Ohio, maybe play Muirfield Village, look at videotapes of his swing now and then. Has also politely let me know that he now prefers the name William. Wonder what Frank Urban "Fuzzy" Zoeller would have to say about that? But of course the kid never heard of Wild Bill Mehlhorn and his cowboy hat at the 1925 PGA. Well: Went nine with him and got skinned. His drives now a sand wedge longer than mine, so I'm hitting my seven wood versus his nine iron or my sixty-yard pitch versus his putt. Waited on the teebox at #7 while some guys in Osh Kosh overalls and seed-company caps yipped their way across the green. Etta laughed and said she just had a recollection of Squeegee saying, Even a really bad day of golf is better than a good day of work. We all grinned like fools. Especially Wild Bill. Hit me that my lame old jokes have always seemed funny and fresh to him. One facet of youth's attractiveness for tiresome gaffers like me. Tried a knock-down five iron to the green, but it whunked into the sand trap. Easy out to within four feet, and then a one-putt for par. Wild Bill missed an opportunity. Etta got lost in the rough with her spoon and scored what the Pro/Am caddies used to say was a "newspaper 8." Walked to the next tee in a garden stroll under an enormous blue sky, just taking everything in, Wild Bill up ahead and my wife next to me and golf the only thing on my mind. And I was everywhere I have ever been: on the public course at age nine with Dad's sawed-down midiron, and again when I was thirteen and parred three in a row, and on my practice round with Tommy Armour and Byron Nelson in 1947, or playing St. Andrews, Oakmont, Winged Foot, Pebble Beach, or here at Sandhills years ago, just hacking around with the guys. Every one was a red-letter day. Etta said, "You're smiling." "Second childhood," said I. Wild Bill played scratch golf after that and then went over to the practice range. Has the passion now. Etta and I went out to the Ponderosa for steak and potatoes on their senior-citizen discount. Have been reading up on Columbus, Ohio, since then. Home of the university, capital of the state, population of 540,000 in 1970, the year that her own Jack Nicklaus won his second British Open.

MAY 30. Went to Holy Sepulchre Cemetery with Etta and put peonies out for the many people we know now interred there. Etta drove me to the course—getting license back Wednesday.

Eugene was there, trying out putters, stinking like turpentine, getting cranky. Went eighteen with me, but only half-decent shot he could manage was a four-wood rouser that Gene Sarazen would have envied. Were joined by a spiffy sales rep from Wilson Sports and Eugene just kept needling him. And a lot of that raunchy talk I don't like. Then hot coffee in the clubhouse. Was asked how long I have been playing the game and said sixty years. Eugene worked out the arithmetic on a paper napkin and the comeuppance was I have spent at least five years of my life on a golf course. "Five years, Cecil! You can't have 'em back. You could've accomplished something important. Ever feel guilty about that?" I sipped from my cup and said, "We're put here for pleasure too." And then we were quiet. Eugene crumpled up the napkin and pitched it across the room. Looking for a topic, I asked how his chemotherapy was playing out, and Eugene said he'd stopped going. Enjoyed my surprise. Said, "What's the point? Huh? You gotta die of somethin'." And I had a picture of Eugene at forty, painting my window sashes, and headstrong and ornery and brimming with vim and vigor. Saddening. Hitched a ride home with him, and Eugene just sat behind the wheel in the driveway, his big hands in his lap, looking at the yard and house paint. "We have all this technology," he said. "Education. High-speed travel. Medical advances. And the twentieth century is still unacceptable." "Well," I said, "at least you've had yourself an adventure." Eugene laughed. Went inside and repaired the hosel on Butch's Cleveland Classic. ($15.) Watched TV. Looked at Nebraska Bar Association mailing about judges under consideration. Have no opinion on the matter. Etta sleeping as I write this. Hope to play nine tomorrow.

Nebraska

The town is Americus, Covenant, Denmark, Grange, Hooray, Jerusalem, Sweetwater—one of the lesser-known moons of the Platte, conceived in sickness and misery by European pioneers who took the path of least resistance and put down roots in an emptiness like the one they kept secret in their youth. In Swedish and Danish and German and Polish, in anxiety and fury and God's providence, they chopped at the Great Plains with spades, creating green sod houses that crumbled and collapsed in the rain and disappeared in the first persuasive snow and were so low the grown-ups stooped to go inside; and yet were places of ownership and a hard kind of happiness, the places their occupants gravely stood before on those plenary occasions when photographs were taken.

And then the Union Pacific stopped by, just a camp of white campaign tents and a boy playing his Harpoon at night, and then a supply store, a depot, a pine water tank, stockyards, and the mean prosperity of the twentieth century. The trains strolling into town to shed a boxcar in the depot sideyard, or crying past at sixty miles per hour, possibly interrupting a girl in her high-wire act, her arms looping up when she tips to one side, the railtop as slippery as a silver spoon. And then the yellow and red locomotive rises up from the heat shimmer over a mile away, the August noonday warping the sight of it, but cinders tapping away from the spikes and the iron rails already vibrating up inside the girl's shoes. She steps down to the roadbed and then into high weeds as the Union Pacific pulls Wyoming coal and Georgia-Pacific lumber and snowplow blades and aslant Japanese pickup trucks through the open countryside and on to Omaha. And when it passes by, a worker she knows is opposite her, like a pedestrian at a stoplight, the sun not letting up, the plainsong of grasshoppers going on and on between them until the worker says, "Hot."

Twice the Union Pacific tracks cross over the sidewinding Democrat, the water slow as an oxcart, green as silage, croplands to the east, yards and houses to the west, a green ceiling of leaves in some places, whirlpools showing up in it like spinning plates that lose speed and disappear. In winter and a week or more of just above zero, high-school couples walk the gray ice, kicking up snow as quiet words are passed between them, opinions are mildly compromised, sorrows are apportioned. And Emil Jedlicka unslings his blue-stocked .22 and slogs through high brown weeds and snow, hunting ring-necked pheasant, sidelong rabbits, and—always suddenly—quail, as his little brother Orin sprints across the Democrat in order to slide like an otter.

July in town is a gray highway and a Ford hay truck spraying by, the hay sailing like a yellow ribbon caught in the mouth of a prancing dog, and Billy Awalt up there on the camel's hump, eighteen years old and sweaty and dirty, peppered and dappled with hay dust, a lump of chew like an extra thumb under his lower lip, his blue eyes happening on a Dairy Queen and a pretty girl licking a pale trickle of ice cream from the cone. And Billy slaps his heart and cries, "Oh! I am pierced!"

And late October is orange on the ground and blue overhead and grain silos stacked up like white poker chips, and a high silver water tower belittled one night by the sloppy tattoo of one year's class at George W. Norris High. And below the silos and water tower are stripped treetops, their gray limbs still lifted up in alleluia, their yellow leaves crowding along yard fences and sheeping along the sidewalks and alleys under the shepherding wind.

Or January and a heavy snow partitioning the landscape, whiting out the highways and woods and cattle lots until there are only open spaces and steamed-up windowpanes, and a Nordstrom boy limping pitifully in the hard plaster of his clothes, the snow as deep as his hips when the boy tips over and cannot get up until a little Schumacher girl sitting by the stoop window, a spoon in her mouth, a bowl of Cheerios in her lap, says in plain voice, "There's a boy," and her mother looks out to the sidewalk.

Houses are big and white and two stories high, each a cousin to the next, with pigeon roosts in the attic gables, green storm windows on the upper floor, and a green screened porch, some as pillowed and couched as parlors or made into sleeping rooms for the boy whose next step will be the Navy and days spent on a ship with his hometown's own population, on gray water that rises up and is allayed like a geography of cornfields, sugar beets, soybeans, wheat, that stays there and says, in its own way, "Stay." Houses are turned away from the land and toward whatever is not always, sitting across from each other like dressed-up children at a party in daylight, their parents looking on with hopes and fond expectations. Overgrown elm and sycamore trees poach the sunlight from the lawns and keep petticoats of snow around them into April. In the deep lots out back are wire clotheslines with flapping white sheets pinned to them, property lines are hedged with sour green and purple grapes, or with rabbit wire and gardens of peonies, roses, gladiola, irises, marigolds, pansies. Fruit trees are so closely planted that they cannot sway without knitting. The apples and cherries drop and sweetly decompose until they're only slight brown bumps in the yards, but the pears stay up in the wind, drooping under the pecks of birds, withering down like peppers until their sorrow is justly noticed and they one day disappear.

Aligned against an alley of blue shale rock is a garage whose doors slash weeds and scrape up pebbles as an old man pokily swings them open, teetering with his last weak push. And then Victor Johnson rummages inside, being cautious about his gray sweater and high-topped shoes, looking over paint cans, junked electric motors, grass rakes and garden rakes and a pitchfork and sickles, gray doors and ladders piled overhead in the rafters, and an old windup Victrola and heavy platter records from the twenties, on one of them a soprano singing "I'm a Lonesome Melody." Under a green tarpaulin is a wooden movie projector he painted silver and big cans of tan celluloid, much of it orange and green with age, but one strip of it preserved: of an Army pilot in jodhpurs hopping from one biplane onto another's upper wing. Country people who'd paid to see the movie had been spellbound by the slight dip of the wings at the pilot's jump, the slap of his leather jacket, and how his hair strayed wild and was promptly sleeked back by the wind. But looking at the strip now, pulling a ribbon of it up to a windowpane and letting it unspool to the ground, Victor can make out only twenty frames of the leap, and then snapshot after snapshot of an Army pilot clinging to the biplane's wing. And yet Victor stays with it, as though that scene of one man staying alive were what he'd paid his nickel for.

Main Street is just a block away. Pickup trucks stop in it so their drivers can angle out over their brown left arms and speak about crops or praise the weather or make up sentences whose only real point is their lack of complication. And then a cattle truck comes up and they mosey along with a touch of their cap bills or a slap of the door metal. High-school girls in skin-tight jeans stay in one place on weekends, and jacked-up cars cruise past, rowdy farmboys overlapping inside, pulling over now and then in order to give the girls cigarettes and sips of pop and grief about their lipstick. And when the cars peel out, the girls say how a particular boy measured up or they swap gossip about Donna Moriarity and the scope she permitted Randy when he came back from boot camp.

Everyone is famous in this town. And everyone is necessary. Townspeople go to the Vaughn Grocery Store for the daily news, and to the Home Restaurant for history class, especially at evensong when the old people eat graveled pot roast and lemon meringue pie and calmly sip coffee from cups they tip to their mouths with both hands. The Kiwanis Club meets here on Tuesday nights, and hopes are made public, petty sins are tidily dispatched, the proceeds from the gumball machines are tallied up and poured into the upkeep of a playground. Yutesler's Hardware has picnic items and kitchen appliances in its one window, in the manner of those prosperous men who would prefer to be known for their hobbies. And there is one crisp, white, Protestant church with a steeple, of the sort pictured on calendars; and the Immaculate Conception Catholic Church, grayly holding the town at bay like a Gothic wolfhound. And there is an insurance agency, a county coroner and justice of the peace, a secondhand shop, a handsome chiropractor named Koch who coaches the Pony League baseball team, a post office approached on unpainted wood steps outside of a cheap mobile home, the Nighthawk tavern where there's Falstaff tap beer, a green pool table, a poster recording the Cornhuskers scores, a crazy man patiently tolerated, a gray-haired woman with an unmoored eye, a boy in spectacles thick as paperweights, a carpenter missing one index finger, a plump waitress whose day job is in a basement beauty shop, an old woman who creeps up to the side door at eight in order to purchase one shot glass of whiskey.

And yet passing by, and paying attention, an outsider is only aware of what isn't, that there's no bookshop, no picture show, no pharmacy or dry cleaners, no cocktail parties, extreme opinions, jewelry or piano stores, motels, hotels, hospital, political headquarters, philosophical theories about Being and the soul.

High importance is only attached to practicalities, and so there is the Batchelor Funeral Home, where a proud old gentleman is on display in a dark brown suit, his yellow fingernails finally clean, his smeared eyeglasses in his coat pocket, a grandchild on tiptoes by the casket, peering at the lips that will not move, the sparrow chest that will not rise. And there's Tommy Seymour's for Sinclair gasoline and mechanical repairs, a green balloon dinosaur bobbing from a string over the cash register, old tires piled beneath the cottonwood, For Sale in the sideyard a Case tractor, a John Deere reaper, a hay mower, a red manure spreader, and a rusty grain conveyor, green weeds overcoming them, standing up inside them, trying slyly and little by little to inherit machinery for the earth.

And beyond that are woods, a slope of pasture, six empty cattle pens, a driveway made of limestone pebbles, and the house where Alice Sorensen pages through a child's World Book Encyclopedia, stopping at the descriptions of California, Capetown, Ceylon, Colorado, Copenhagen, Corpus Christi, Costa Rica, Cyprus.

Widow Dworak has been watering the lawn in an open raincoat and apron, but at nine she walks the green hose around to the spigot and screws down the nozzle so that the spray is a misty crystal bowl softly baptizing the ivy. She says, "How about some camomile tea?" And she says, "Yum. Oh, boy. That hits the spot." And bends to shut the water off.

The Union Pacific night train rolls through town just after ten o'clock when a sixty-year-old man named Adolf Schooley is a boy again in bed, and when the huge weight of forty or fifty cars jostles his upstairs room like a motor he'd put a quarter in. And over the sighing industry of the train, he can hear the train saying *Nebraska, Nebraska, Nebraska, Nebraska.* And he cannot sleep.

Mrs. Antoinette Heft is at the Home Restaurant, placing frozen meat patties on waxed paper, pausing at times to clamp her fingers under her arms and press the sting from them. She stops when the Union Pacific passes, then picks a cigarette out of a pack of Kools and smokes it on the back porch, smelling air as crisp as Oxydol, looking up at stars the Pawnee Indians looked at, hearing the low harmonica of big rigs on the highway, in the town she knows like the palm of her hand, in the country she knows by heart.